WAITING FOR
TOMORROW

Also available in English from Graywolf Press

The Last Brother

WAITING FOR TOMORROW

A NOVEL

Nathacha Appanah

*Translated from the French
by Geoffrey Strachan*

GRAYWOLF PRESS

This publication is made possible, in part, by the voters of Minnesota through a Minnesota State Arts Board Operating Support grant, thanks to a legislative appropriation from the arts and cultural heritage fund, and a grant from the Wells Fargo Foundation. Significant support has also been provided by the National Endowment for the Arts, Target, the McKnight Foundation, the Lannan Foundation, the Amazon Literary Partnership, and other generous contributions from foundations, corporations, and individuals. To these organizations and individuals we offer our heartfelt thanks.

Special funding for this title was provided by Edwin C. Cohen.

Published by Graywolf Press
250 Third Avenue North, Suite 600
Minneapolis, Minnesota 55401

www.graywolfpress.org

Published in the United States of America

ISBN 978-1-55597-803-7

2 4 6 8 9 7 5 3 1
First Graywolf Printing, 2018

Library of Congress Control Number: 2017938027

Cover design and illustration: Kimberly Glyder Design

*For Bernard Gouley
and Clotilde Monteiro*

CONTENTS

PART THREE

WAITING FOR
TOMORROW

Today

DAWN BREAKS OVER THE HORIZON. IT MOVES ACROSS THE SEA, SOAR-
ing over the empty beach where Anita and Adèle had sat one
festive evening, climbing up silently through the city, slipping
along without pausing in the street where, at number seven, a
children's shoe store has taken the place of Adam's architectural
office. It reaches the top of the hill and lingers there, gray and
hazy for a moment, before suddenly plunging down the far side.
It sweeps over houses, streets, trees, and flowers asleep on balconies. Down in the valleys it seems to dance, lightly, discreetly.
It seeps into the forest and spills across the lake where no one
ventures now since Adèle drowned there four years, five months,
and thirteen days ago.

The dawn finds Anita in her kitchen, seated at a great wooden
table, with her back to the broad bay windows through which, for
several minutes more, a few stars can be seen in the sky. Anita is
wearing a long turquoise skirt, its hem now frayed by wear, and
a gray pullover that belongs to her husband, Adam. She has had
a sleepless night. She has been thinking about the old days, remembering forgotten dreams, things left undone, she has tried
to look into her heart, she has been thinking about Adèle. Sitting
there, barefoot, her eyes red, Anita is waiting for day finally to
break, with a dry crack like the tough, wrinkled shell of a walnut.

The morning light slips slowly across the living room and enters the bedroom where Laura, Anita and Adam's daughter, is

asleep. At this moment Laura is dreaming that she is swimming in the lake. It is a dream she often has, she runs along the jetty to give herself momentum, takes off, and performs a perfect swan dive. Her strokes are graceful, almost soundless, as if Laura were made of water. Those of her father, whose presence she senses close beside her, are noisy and powerful. Adèle is in this dream too, but she is swimming beneath her, completely underwater. It is a strange sensation but not unpleasant. Laura feels as though she is surrounded, supported. In her dream Laura has forgotten that for the past four years, five months, and thirteen days she has been unable either to run or to perform swan dives, or to swim.

The dawn bathes the house and the forest in a dove gray color and makes its way across fields and mountain villages. When it reaches the front of the prison complex surrounded by barbed wire, Adam is on his feet, his face pressed against the little window, gripping the bars with both hands. Just now, when he climbed onto the table to reach the opening, he recalled the traditional French name for windows set high in the wall: they are known as *jours de souffrance*, "dark days." Adam is waiting for the dawn, as he has been waiting for his release for four years, five months, and thirteen days. He has had a sleepless night, he has been thinking about the old days, all those promises not kept, the dozens of little acts of cowardice one scatters in one's path. He has been thinking about Adèle. Now Adam stands there, barefoot, and at last he is looking the dawn in the eye.

PART ONE

A New Year's Eve party

TWENTY YEARS EARLIER IN A TRADITIONAL SOLID BRICK HOUSE IN Montreuil, on the eastern outskirts of Paris, Adam and Anita are perched on a vast, deep sofa covered in green velvet. A pile of clothes lies between them—coats, jackets, sweaters, scarves, hats, gloves—and as yet each is unaware of the other's presence. It is the last half hour of the old year, it is still the twentieth century, they are both twenty-four. They are each haunted by a sense of failure, the feeling that, somehow or other, they have once more got it wrong, they should have been braver, less sensitive, less themselves. Later on, when people ask them how they met, they will reply (in unison), *it was all thanks to a green sofa.*

But not so fast.

Before he ended up on the sofa Adam had been in the dining room converted into a dance floor and bar where the only drink was a highly alcoholic punch. It was his first New Year's Eve in Paris. Until now he had always gone home for the holidays, returning to his life as woodcutter / cabinetmaker / painter / surfer / marathon runner / only son. Every year he would be amazed by the ease, the pleasure, and the relief with which he reverted to being that Adam, a rugged, energetic young man, who smelled of timber and salt, and was given to deep breathing and outbursts of hearty laughter. He would also have the feeling he still cannot find words to express, a mixture of enthusiasm and relief welling up once the first pine trees have been spotted beside the *route nationale*, the tops of the trees silhouetted against the dusk sky, the russet color the ferns turn to in winter, the pounding of the waves that he hears before seeing the sea.

Every year, it is true, he was bracing himself to experience the feelings that seemed to be common to all of his new friends, that boredom with home life, that distaste for the provinces, that contempt for the countryside, in short, the dreary prospect of being far away from the city and with their parents. But on the threshold of the wooden house his father had built with his own hands, his whole being would be overcome by a soft, warm sensation, in which he felt happy, at ease, safe. Adam liked being at home, he liked his father's company, he went running in the forest with his friend Imran, a marathon runner like himself, he swam and surfed, he painted. Adam liked the simplicity of what it was to be a man down there. Sometimes he felt ashamed as well. Was he making the most of his youth? Wasn't he just a big spoiled child? Shouldn't he be yearning for something more (travel, action, noise, city lights, passion)?

For this New Year holiday Adam had decided to stay in Paris. It was his fifth and last year at the school of architecture. Here is what he would do: a long stroll through the city, taking in the most brilliantly lit streets, the most imposing bridges, the grandest squares, the most impressive monuments. He would study all the plaques, go into churches, sit on public benches. Then he would walk up the Champs-Élysées and lay a flower on the tomb of the unknown soldier in memory of his great-grandfather, André, who had died at Soissons in 1917. As midnight began to strike somewhere, he would be beneath the Arc de Triomphe and it would be perfect.

But at the last minute Adam had abandoned the whole plan because his friend Paul had laughed and said to him: *What? You're going to lay a flower on the tomb of the unknown soldier on New Year's Eve? You must be joking!*

Behind this Adam had sensed more, things not said out loud

but conveyed in a raised eyebrow, an ironic smile: *You're just a peasant, get back to your farm.*

In a world in which Adam had had sufficient self-confidence here is what he would have explained:

André, a *"poilu,"* a French soldier killed in fighting at Soissons in 1917, the father of Maurice, a resistance fighter, killed in a bombing raid in Bordeaux in 1944, the father of André, pine tree tapper and woodcutter, born in 1940 in Hossegor in the Basque country, the father of Adam.

In a world in which Adam did not feel inferior because he is a provincial, here is what he would have described:

Evenings in the wooden house where the talk is of those heroes. André, who died in the mud, and Maurice, killed at Bordeaux on a patch of wasteland. The sticky gray mud, the rats on André's body, the dark snow falling heavily on that endless night in 1917. Maurice's blood caught up in the vegetation that morning in '44, the dandelion clock blown apart by the draft from his body. Adam's wax crayon drawings of the tufted herons taking flight gently, ever so gently, the wind that morning is just a light breeze.

But Adam had not come out with any of this. He had laughed as well, and agreed to spend the evening in Montreuil. Beneath his heart, he felt a pain like that from the point of a dagger, just like what he used to feel when running a marathon, around the twelfth mile, and what he heard at that moment was: *Foreigner!* Who had said that? Had this word been lurking among Paul's splutterings?

At the start of the evening in that house in Montreuil, Adam thinks he'll get used to it all, of course he will, he's twenty-four years old, for God's sake! There is music, pretty girls with glittering makeup, laughter everywhere. But the hours pass and Adam feels he is shrinking, wilting. He stays on his own in a corner, in his bubble, like a foreigner who does not speak the same language as the others, does not understand their rituals, their culture.

Adam thinks about his father back home in their house. Has it snowed in the valley? What are the waves like tonight? He thinks about his surfboard. Oh, the thrill of tucking it under his arm, and running into the water, that unbelievable thrill! He tries to call to mind the smell of the room where he paints, imagines himself settling down on the stool, patient and alert in front of a white canvas. He knows a secret lies hidden there that he has never yet truly grasped.

Now Adam pictures himself floating above all these people about whom he doesn't give a damn, students of law, architecture, psychology, literature. He goes flying out through the window, out into the cold and the snow, toward the Arc de Triomphe, toward the flame, toward his great-grandfather. Ever since he has been in Paris he has wanted to do this, but he has been waiting for a special day, for he wanted to remember it always, to do it in such a way that later, on a winter's evening, he could, in his turn, begin a story with words something like this: *I spent the first minutes of the New Year beneath the Arc de Triomphe, beside the flame of the unknown soldier.* Adam has always been fond of stories.

Liar! Who said that?

What is the matter with him? His whole body begins to shake. Adam staggers out of the noisy room, passes through the kitchen, walks along a corridor, finds himself in a dimly lit room. At the end of it a sofa piled high with coats. He dives onto it, head first, his body curled into a ball, with both the determination of someone plunging into a melee and the desperation of someone longing to return into his mother's womb. Adam, half man, half child, that is how he settles onto the sofa, his neck at an angle, like a duck sheltering under its own wing, his chin on his knees, his hands clasping his ankles.

It is here that the dagger pricks him most deeply, here that the two words, *Foreigner* and *Liar*, make themselves clearly heard, and with them a mass of details crowds in: his regional accent, which he tries hard to smooth over since he is so sick of people asking him where he comes from (Belgium? Switzerland? Canada?);

the endless waiting for some surge of enthusiasm that never arrives (just look at that avenue! that light! that dome! that face! those legs! that energy!); his studies, at which he turns out to be merely average, after having always been top of his class; his vain efforts to be like everyone else, up to the minute, in fashion, a smoker, a drinker, a nonstop talker, a womanizer, isn't that what being young is all about? Adam used to think that here in this city he would be transformed into a more sophisticated, more intelligent, and more ambitious version of himself. He believed he would be inspired by the centuries-old paved streets, the monuments, the gardens, the flights of steps leading to romantic squares, the cabaret theaters, the songs, the brasseries, the hundreds of thousands of people going down into the metro every morning, the woman from next door laying a hand lightly on his chest as she speaks to him, the milliner's store at the end of the street, the perfect chocolate cream puff, the white and gold carousel, the folded metro ticket at the bottom of his pocket.

In his brain (that creature with a thousand lights, portals, hiding places, and passageways) a notion arises and offers Adam the solace of truth.

I don't belong here.

I don't belong here.

I don't belong here.

Adam becomes aware that he is repeating this sentence out loud only when the pile of coats replies to him:

"Welcome to the club, my friend."

Anita is sitting, or rather crouching, hugging her upraised legs, head lowered, forehead resting on her knees, inhaling her own warm vanilla scent. There has been substantial traffic since she took refuge here. People walk in, dump their stuff on the pile that is already quite high or on top of her, and go out, laughing. Everyone is laughing this evening, animated by an unrelenting collective gaiety. This is how the new year must discover us when it arrives; sparkling eyes, open mouths, glass in hand, arm around a friend, body gyrating. Better that than huddled up on a green sofa, all alone and buried under a pile of coats.

And yet it had all started well. She had arrived with Christophe and they had been kissing. But when he had tried to slip his hand under her skirt she had slapped his face. Oh yes, it had been a real good slap, swift, hard, impossible to dodge. It had been a reflex action—and yet for such an action to occur doesn't there have to be thought, a connection made, the alerting of the nervous system, the transmission of data? There was just that sudden impulse in her right hand, arising more or less at the level of her wrist ("an impulse arose," that's something she ought to write down in her notebook, where she writes things down, words, phrases, ideas for use later, in, shh, *the novel*). At the very moment when her hand was striking that boy's cheek, she was once again astonished at the girl she had become. In the old days she would never have slapped him. She would have resisted, wriggling this way and that (in her mind's eye she sees her place being taken by a fine silvery gray fish in Christophe's grasp, he leans forward, his mouth half open, concentrating on his catch), she would have uttered frightened little squeals and her eyes would have filled with tears.

But here, in this city, Anita has become high-strung, impulsive, often filled with bitter anger. Once she used to write neatly turned, well-rhymed things, charming verses (the way you might knit a charming sweater, arrange a charming bouquet). She wrote what she saw: *a bird on a branch, an innocent blue sky . . .* and she won prizes for her poetry. She dressed in pastel shades and plaited her black hair into delicate braids.

Now jagged words well up inside her, arranging themselves almost involuntarily into poems that are published in a well-regarded literary magazine that sells few copies and is edited by François Sol. Thrilling poems, François Sol had said to her, some months previously, laying a hand on her arm. Anita is afraid of

François Sol, his office piled high with editions of classic writers published in the Pléiade series, anthologies, complete works, rare editions, his formal manner of speaking that seems like a putdown, the way he tosses a volume of Nietzsche or Kierkegaard or a copy of *Ulysses* nonchalantly onto the top of a pile, his questions and the advice that follows without his waiting for an answer to the question. (Have you read Joyce? You must read Joyce. Do you keep a diary? You must keep a diary.) The truth is that she dreads him examining her properly, with his gecko-green eyes, dreads him unmasking her beneath her heavy makeup, her military boots, and her hair bound tight, like a sailor's knot, dreads him seeing beyond her vitriolic poems, beyond her gear, and dismissing her with vexing bluntness, a finger pointed at the door, the way one dismisses an imposter.

Five years ago she was still that young girl (*a bird on a branch, an innocent blue sky*) when she arrived in this city and a distant cousin met her at the airport and took her to her home, on the twenty-fourth floor of a tower block in the suburb of Rosny. Anita stayed for a week, the time it took for the promised room on the university campus to become free. There were sharp corners everywhere in her cousin's apartment (little square rooms opening onto other rectangular spaces), and it was decorated with plastic flowers and pictures in relief representing scenes (ranging from the Eiffel Tower to the Arc de Triomphe). Everywhere a heavy scent of incense and spices. In this apartment, during the first few moments, as her mind and body took in this new setting that was as dismal as it was unexpected, Anita had wanted to become a child again, so that she could scream and weep and roll on the ground. An unbelievably powerful feeling overcame her when she thought about her parents, their house close to the sea, the spacious rooms flooded with light, the red waxed floor, the garden, their dog who was called Dog, the wide veranda where, as a child, she used to measure the progress of the dawning sun with her school ruler. It was a mixture of nostalgia, sadness, desire, lack, a profound longing to be elsewhere—for the first time Anita was experiencing homesickness.

This cousin of hers, a woman who worked at night and slept by day, was afraid of everything: blacks, Sri Lankans, Romanians, motorbikes, young people, elderly whites pulling their shopping carts in the mornings, dogs, and the full moon. Anita remained a prisoner in that apartment for a week and it was there she wrote her first "New Poem." There was no bird now, no blue sky. Instead grayness, metal, sulfur, bitter smells. The very things that François Sol finds thrilling.

Just now, having slapped that boy, having seen him put his hand to his cheek with a theatrically questioning look in his eyes (*et tu, Anita?*), she had muttered some words of apology and locked herself in the bathroom.

What is the matter with her? After all, she had been eager to come with Christophe that evening, she had drunk two glasses of the excessively strong punch, she had danced, she had thought about her parents, a notion that had swollen like a balloon in her stomach, colliding gently with her heart, making her want to cry. She had kissed Christophe. She liked him (a pleasant feeling that did not take up too much space within her) but then she had ruined everything. She would have liked to be able to explain to him, run past him again the film of them fondling one another and then stop it at precisely the moment when Christophe's hand slides up under her skirt and she becomes the incarnation of the phrase *simply in self-defense*. I didn't *mean* to do it, she would explain, it was just a reflex.

Anita looks around the bathroom. She does not know it yet, but this is her strength, she knows how to look: color, shade, shape, appearance, material, shadow, light, precise terms for things (mixer faucet, pedestal washbowl). Diverse objects (a large green plastic apple for storing cotton balls) take their places in a corner of her brain (that creature with a thousand lights, portals, hiding places, and passageways), go into hibernation, and are later reborn in a short story, a poem, the draft for a novel, an article.

She stands up, catches her reflection in the mirror. If she turns her head to the left she will see her father; if she screws up her eyes and smiles, she will encounter her mother's features. She would so much like to be spending this New Year's Eve with them, to be sitting on the veranda looking across at her parents. They would be listening to the radio, they would be reading, her mother would have gotten the three glasses ready, and the bottle of sparkling wine, her father would have taken out the fireworks for them to set off at midnight. What is the sky like on the other side of the world? How are the stars shining? Are her parents thinking of her at this very moment?

A bird on a branch, an innocent blue sky.

No, of course, she has no desire to become that Anita again (she thinks about herself as of a child, tenderly). But she would like to cease being what she is now, this girl forever rushing in, exaggerating her features, violating language. She washes her face vigorously with soap, rinses it with cold water, and spreads a dab of Nivea cream, found in the cupboard above the bath-tub, over her skin. She looks at herself and on her face there is a hint of what she once was. Her eyes grow misty with tears. Homesickness overcomes her again.

Escape.

Anita needs to escape. She feels unwell. She staggers out of the bathroom, the music seems to be erupting on all sides, she is looking for the exit. She is looking for her coat. She does not want to go onto the dance floor, she collides with bodies (Watch out, Anita! she hears). She shrinks away and ends up on a sofa. She buries herself beneath the pile of garments, covers her ears, she'd just like to hear a jazz tune played on the piano, for a long time she does not stir.

Until.

I don't belong here.

Yes, that's it. That's it precisely.

It takes her a few seconds to realize that she was not the one who had said it (she thought it was the voice *inside* her head). There is someone else on the sofa. And this person says it again.

I don't belong here.

Before the new year discovers them locked in an unexpected embrace that will turn out to be amazingly sweet and delicious (Adam will think of his father, of their wooden house, of the silence of the forest on a snowy night, he will like her scent of vanilla and freshness; Anita will think of her parents, a jazz tune on a piano, she will like his scent of timber and salt: they will feel good), before the countdown to midnight is yelled by everybody at the tops of their voices, at the other end of the house, before they look at one another for the first time, she will finally smile at that repeated "I don't belong here" and will reply:

Welcome to the club, my friend.

An oddly matched couple

YOU COULD CALL THEM AN ODDLY MATCHED COUPLE. HE IS VERY tall with fine chestnut-colored hair that turns gold in sunlight. His body is slim, knotty in places, and his long-distance-runner's legs are superb. His face is fairly ordinary but there is something in his gaze that inspires trust, an openness, a show of innocence. She is petite with black hair that reaches to her waist. Her face is round, the color of gingerbread, her skin is as smooth as a baby's, her brow is wide, her eyes shine when she speaks. She does not know how to swim, he does not know how to climb trees. He loves rugby, she does not begin to understand it. He talks to her about the "*poilus*" in the trenches, the resistance, about André and Maurice, his absolute heroes; she tells him the story of her great-grandfather arriving on the island of Mauritius to take over from the slaves on the sugar plantations. She finds it unthinkable that anyone could eat headcheese, he finds it unthinkable that anyone should eat hot peppers; he finds the expression "a woman of color" quite charming, she thinks it is the language of colonialism; he does not know what a banyan is, she would not recognize a stone pine.

They live in a studio apartment on the third floor of a squat building behind the Gare du Nord train station. The walls are vivid yellow. Each has a corner to work in. Over here an easel, a stool, tubes of paint, palettes, brushes, canvases, over there a desk, notebooks, books, pens. They are amazed at how they are able to work and create side by side. They are convinced that this rare ease is one of the reasons why they have made the right choice, one that will endure and flourish.

In summer the light bounces off the yellow walls and the two of them feel as if they are living inside the sun itself. They make love on the floor, they fall asleep almost naked on a quilt decorated with images of the setting sun, a fisherman, and a leaping swordfish, with perfectly arched sprays of water.

But summer is far away now. This is early January and freezing rain is falling outside. Anita wakes up. A certain haziness envelops her, something rather like a blurred photograph. It is that special moment, delicate and fleeting, between night and the early hours before dawn. Anita places a hand upon her stomach. She is pregnant.

From time to time bursts of freezing rain beat against the window. Anita thinks the sound resembles that made by the first drops of rain on a corrugated tin roof, but she is not certain. This doubt causes her to frown—she is used to memories, comparisons, and parallels flooding in easily, she is used to her mind functioning swiftly and well, to it traveling to and fro between here, this city, and back there, that island. Since she left Mauritius almost ten years ago, she has returned to her island only once, she went with Adam. That was three months ago, her father, Philip, had just died. For thirteen days Anita did not say a word to Adam, did not weep, and asked only questions of her mother. She would rise at dawn, take her shower, gulp down a cup of tea, and go out. Because she had not been able to see him, to touch him, because the mound of the grave, the white cross, the plants in pots, were not her father, Anita wanted to comprehend everything. She opened a new notebook and embarked on a long, exhausting investigation. She questioned her mother, the neighbors, the priest, the fisherman, Alphonse, who had found her father's body, policemen, her mother all over again. She covered page after page with her tiny, tightly compressed handwriting. She spent almost two weeks dissecting seconds, fitting minutes together, going back over gestures, analyzing actions, stopping time. She worked like a laboratory technician, split second by split second. She wanted to know how a man who wakes at 5:00 every morning and has followed the same rituals for decades (hot lemon juice, thirty minutes of yoga, fifteen minutes of exercises, a cold shower, breakfast on the veranda with his wife) can die like a dog in the gutter, one Sunday morning on his way to 7:00 mass.

Philip had chosen to wear chocolate-colored pants and the white shirt with the Mao collar he was particularly fond of. He had put on moccasins and was wearing his beige panama hat with a ribbed hatband the color of tobacco. His elegance had not stopped him being mown down by a huge vehicle (a truck or a bus, no one can confirm this, but a lot of people heard a metallic clatter and the sound of a rusty engine) between 6:50—the time at which he had left the house—and 7:05, when the fisherman Alphonse had found him in the gutter. He still had his moccasins on his feet but his panama hat was found several yards away.

Anita had read and reread her notes until she knew them by heart. She had visualized everything, ticked all the boxes, in the hope of filling the empty spaces in her head and her heart, but she would never know everything.

She would never know how her father had observed the dawn slowly rising above the eucalyptus and mango trees. She would never know how much he had thought about her when the sunlight glowed on the dahlias, the zinnias, the hollyhocks, the pansies, the orange crocuses, the snapdragons, the viburnum, the frangipani tree, the arbor covered in white bougainvillea, the three steps leading to the veranda, the dog. She would never know what his last thoughts were before that terrible roar obliterated everything.

On the fourteenth day, she came back home and called out to her mother, who did not hear her. Then she went into her parents' bedroom and there, placed on her father's desk, she saw the panama hat for the first time. Something gave way within her and she began screaming.

Sarita, her mother, was under the mango tree, comfortably ensconced in an old wicker rocking chair, and was watching Adam repairing the other four armchairs in the set. She and Philip had bought this furniture long before Anita's birth, long before sofas covered in velvet or leatherette had begun to fill up living rooms. The previous day Adam had spent long hours with the village carpenter and now he was scraping, varnishing, adding strips of bamboo to the bases, strengthening the legs with scraps of wood. He worked with a dexterity that his stature would never have led one to expect. His big hands, his broad shoulders, his immense legs—how did he manage to coordinate them with this mixture of grace, efficacy, and intelligence? He had dyed two bundles of raffia with indigo blue (he had told her that in French this was also called Indian blue)—what was he going to do with it? Sarita watched him with that mixture of wonder, nervousness, and curiosity normally reserved for newborn babies. During the previous thirteen days Adam had been discreetly taking things in hand: repairing the drainpipe; rubbing down the wooden balustrade on the veranda and painting it red; oiling the entrance gate; trimming the bamboo hedge; pruning the bougainvilleas; digging out weeds; mowing the lawn; fitting new padlocks; cleaning out and repainting Dog's kennel. He would start in the morning, once Anita had gone out, and he worked with assurance, unhurriedly, as if he had always been familiar with the local materials, the local ways of doing things, the local flowers and plants. At first Sarita followed him with her eyes and kept her distance, then she would venture an opinion (red rather than blue for the veranda), a piece of advice (better to buy the padlocks at the second hardware store rather than the first). Finally she would go up to him to give encouragement, to offer him a drink, to ask him if he preferred his fish well fried or just lightly, to suggest that he have a rest, go swimming, take a walk. She was aware, even as she counted off the minutes, hours, and days that now lay between her and her husband, even though in the evenings a great gulf of grief and loneliness opened up, even though despair and helplessness overwhelmed her when she saw Anita going out every morning, she was aware of the good this young man was doing her.

Sarita and Adam were in the garden when they heard Anita's cry. They looked at one another but were not surprised. Simply relieved. They had never mentioned it, but while Anita was going through the same actions over and over again, following the same path back and forth, asking the same questions again and again, reading and rereading her notes, the two of them, each in their own way, in their heads, in their hearts, were waiting for her grief to come, for her tears to flow, as one waits for a ripe fruit to fall of its own accord.

As Sarita went into the house to take her daughter in her arms at last, Adam went back to work. He threaded the strands of raffia in and out of the bamboo, and caught himself thinking that he was using the same actions here, on the shores of the Indian Ocean, as his father, when he was repairing the tarpaulin that protected his supply of logs back at home, on the shores of the Atlantic. This notion gave him a pleasant feeling of fulfillment. He felt rooted in the earth—over here or back there, it was all the same. As his hands worked without stopping, following the blue raffia, in, out, in, out, the notion itself was embodied within them, and it was as if he were working with water, sand, salt, earth, wind, and sky.

Later on, during the night, Sarita heard the floor creak. Something infinitely discreet like a grasshopper's feet on a mango leaf. Sarita recognized her daughter's footsteps as she went to be with Adam in his room (the same tiny sound as when, in childhood, she had gone to finish off the chocolate cake in the fridge or to wait outside the door for Santa Claus). She smiled.

Three months later, in her bed, Anita is breathing deeply. She no longer wants to weep for her father, for the time being she no longer wants to think about her island. There is this new life making itself known, this warm and sweet aspect of existence, she wants to concentrate on what she oddly visualizes as a kidney bean in her lower belly . . . She forgets about the sound of the freezing rain, which may or may not resemble the first drops falling on a corrugated tin roof.

Without Anita being aware of it, the minor memories of her homeland are slowly fading—those intimate details that linger not in the head, but on the skin and in the pit of the stomach: the exact color of the sugarcane flowers in June, the sensation of perfectly cooked rice in one's mouth, the taste of a water ice or a syrup ice, the sound of rain on a corrugated tin roof.

Anita is twenty-nine and she has agreed to leave Paris to go and settle in the region where Adam lived as a child. She will not finish her internship in the editorial department of a women's magazine, she will no longer hear the metal shutters grinding open at the grocery at 7:00 in the morning, she will no longer attend monthly lectures on philosophy in the bookstore on the rue des Écoles (near the Sorbonne), she will never be that nervous, aspiring writer arriving on foot to deliver her manuscript, no longer will she go to eat an Indian thali up near the Gare du Nord, nor join the queue for free entry to a museum on the first Sunday of the month, along with the students, penniless dreamers, impoverished intellectuals, and lonely old teachers. But isn't it a kind of immaturity, to be thinking about such things, such minutiae, when you are being given the opportunity to make a fresh start in life? A wooden house designed by the man you love, marriage, a child! Anita bridles at this unwelcome notion, shot through as it is with guilt at submitting to tradition, to Adam, to motherhood, to the law of nature. She bridles at the prospect of becoming a woman like so many others.

Anita turns toward Adam and is touched once more by his way of sleeping, his body straight, his knees slightly bent, both hands folded beneath his ear, his back toward her. Soon this great body she cherishes will spring into action but every night there he is, as if laid gently upon the bed, and in the morning, for several minutes, there is this perfect imprint upon the sheets. Why does she believe she does not completely deserve this man who is so tall, so responsible, so reassuring, so appealing? She thinks back to that New Year's Eve five years ago (their frantic dash out of the house in Montreuil, wearing clothes that were not their own, a black fake fur overcoat, a woolen jacket the color of tobacco, a green scarf, a gray hat, a houndstooth-checked cap; that marvelous moment beneath the Arc de Triomphe), and reflects that it will make a good story to tell this little kidney bean. Nothing else really matters, does it? She will be able to return to work with some local publishing company. She will have a real study and time, at last, to write a novel, she will be able to go strolling through the forest or at the water's edge. A soft warmth envelopes her. Reassured, Anita goes back to sleep.

A few minutes later Adam opens his eyes in his turn and looks around abruptly. Why is he so afraid that Anita may disappear from his life as suddenly as she appeared in it? All at once he thinks of their trip to Mauritius three months before and of that incredible night when Anita had finally gone to be with him in his room. He had woken up with the feeling of a body stretching out alongside his own, of a slim warm arm slipping over his stomach. Anita had loved him differently that night. Before that there had always been something she held back, a physical shyness he had learned to accept, but that night she had not closed her eyes, her gaze was open and frank. She was at home, she was within herself, as he was in her, too. She spoke to him in a new way, very softly, in his ear. And that caused a little explosion within him, one that set off colored fountains and brilliant lights for a long, long time.

Adam studies Anita as she sleeps, her hands folded over her stomach, and a marvelous feeling of well-being steals over him.

That's it! They are leaving Paris! They are expecting a child! No longer will Adam wake up in the middle of the night feverish and uneasy. He has had enough of the badly paid work in that architectural office. All the time tidying up sketches, limply taking part in the rearranging of a middle-class living room, estimating costs, finding solutions that provided what were called "good spatial connections." Every day Adam devoted a disproportionate and perfectly useless amount of energy to fitting into the complex mechanism that is the office, there among the men, women, things, ambitions, desires, and backbiting. He knows he will never quite manage it. He is not outgoing, flamboyant, ambitious enough. His stature is an illusion. He is much too old-fashioned, too shy. Now that they have made the decision to move, Adam is happy. He can visualize perfectly the house he is going to build at the edge of the forest on the Atlantic shore. A wooden structure located in a clearing, a simple cube, with a veranda at the front, broad bay windows set in dark iron frames that will offer views of the forest in rectangular segments like a series of natural pictures. A red floor with broad planks for the veranda, a big farm table in the kitchen, a study for Anita on the western side, a vegetable garden, fruit trees, a studio for himself, apart from the house. Yes, he will finally be that Adam, the one he has always wanted to be, a man who designs his own house, who chooses the timber, the nails, the colors, the curvature of the staircases, a man who fashions the furniture where his child will sleep, where his wife will work, from which they will eat as a family. A man who will sustain his home, with all his strength and intelligence, and who, at his office in the town, will design other houses, other places of work, other structures that bring people together, an old-fashioned man, yes, and one who will keep a low profile alongside the talents of his wife (a poet! a journalist!), alongside her special, exotic beauty. Adam is strong, he feels invincible. He has the impression that the space he occupies in the world is growing, his size is asserting itself, and all this, far from choking him, reassures him. He is an ancient tree, his roots deeply embedded in the earth, his branches thrust high into the sky, casting a broad and reassuring shadow. Adam is, in short, a man. He goes back to sleep, satisfied.

Some months later he is walking along the road that leads to his house. His footfalls are muted by pine needles, sand, and piles of grass. As he often does, Adam is scanning the forest edge on the lookout for a pinecone. He does not know why but for as long as he can remember he has always kept a sharp lookout for the perfect pinecone. If anyone had asked him to describe it he would not have been able to do so, he simply knows that in its color, its shape, the angle of the scales, the weight of it in the hand, the combination of rough and smooth to the touch, he would find in it what for him was the incarnation of perfection. He inhales deeply the smell he loves so much, a mixture of mown grass, salt spray, sweet sap, and freshly turned earth. Adam is home. He is joining his wife, whom he married two hours earlier at the town hall, his father, a few friends. He reaches the end of the path and the house is exactly as he had dreamed it. He has succeeded. Are not his hands more callused? Is not his back still aching? Is not his skin more deeply furrowed, like that of the people from these parts, like that of his father, who had also long ago built his house with his own hands? Adam remembers how, as a child, he loved to spend time on the construction site for their house while it was being built, playing amid all the tools, the freshly dug earth, the noise of the machinery, the masculine talk of the workmen. André, his father, never made a big song and dance about that house, he spoke about it as if it were something very simple to do: to be able to fit together logs, planks, rafters, beams, and tiles and shape them into something that holds together, that lasts and endures.

Adam hears music, laughter, he hears Anita calling him. He has pins and needles in his legs, and a bounding heart, he wants to run up to her, to take her in his arms, to fly with her, to swallow her whole, her and the child, don't they say that to love is to consume? But here she comes now, his wife (my wife! my wife! he says over and over again in his head, as if he had won the lottery, as if something extraordinary had happened to him). Wearing a pearl-gray silk dress, tight bodice, flowing skirt, round belly. She has let down her curly hair, which reaches to her waist. She had said she did not want flowers but had changed her mind at the last minute and had stopped on the way to gather wildflowers, which she has pinned here and there into her hair. She smiles at him, and holds out her hands. They are a happy couple who firmly believe that all their dreams have come true.

"It's the wedding cake moment," she says with a laugh.

"Now it's up to us."

Anita takes his hands and looks at him solemnly.

"Yes, it's up to us now."

The studio apartment with its vivid yellow walls is just a memory. The city is far away. The island is far away. Childhood is over. We are in spring, on the Atlantic shore, where the pine forests come to a halt at the foot of the sand dunes. In a little while Adam and Anita will take a walk along the vast, broad beach that looks as if it were made from the gold of the sunset. In a few weeks' time their daughter, Laura, will be born. Yes, now, more than ever, it is up to them.

A stay-at-home mother

ANITA IS THIRTY-TWO. SHE IS AS LIGHT AS A FEATHER, WITH ALL
the delicacy and competence of a perfect homemaker. She has set
up a big table in the garden and covered it with what is known
as a "Basque" tablecloth—white with red stripes. Since living
in the country she has learned the names of these unfamiliar—
and even strange—things. Basque tablecloth, Gien porcelain,
Louis XV armchair, land left fallow, smoothing timber, national
forest versus locally owned forest, cyclamen flowers, stone pines,
reeds, sedges, *cépage* grapes, frog ponds, land breezes, *"saints de
glace"* (Saints Mamert, Gervase, and Pancras, on whose saints'
days, May 11, 12, and 13, late frosts often occur). When she iden-
tifies these things, or, better still, when she succeeds in incorpo-
rating them into the decor of her daily life, or mentioning them in
a sentence, she feels proud.

Nothing escapes her, so strong is her desire to be of the here
and now. It is not that she has forgotten her own country, her culture, and her traditions, but she dreads being frowned on as un-
cultured, ignorant, foreign. She reads, she absorbs, she observes.
She would like to be able to answer any question her daughter,
Laura, might ask her, to be able to give her the correct names
of plants, birds, insects, to say to her tirelessly *look, listen*. Look,
that is the *eguzkilore*, the wild cactus flower, the flower of the sun.
Listen to the blue tit, come and look at the firebug on the wild
rose. She wages relentless war on her foreign accent. It creeps in

when she is tired and as soon as its sibilant undertones can be heard in what she is saying, she takes the start of each sentence slowly, sits up straight, is extra vigilant about her dropped *r*'s and those ends of sentences left trailing, and the genders of French nouns when they become hazy ("*le manche*," a handle; "*la manche*," a sleeve; "*le poêle*," a stove; "*la poêle*," a frying pan).

Anita has hung a banner between the cherry tree laden with gleaming red but terribly tart fruit and the lilac tree with its delicately perfumed clusters of flowers.

Happy Birthday Laura.

It is early summer and their daughter is about to celebrate her second birthday. Two cakes are baking in the oven—one chocolate, the other vanilla. Anita routinely wipes the table, rearranges the racks where the cakes will cool. She has put in orangeade and apple juice to chill. She has already made a lemon cake for the grownups and iced it. The sink is clean, but she rinses it. She checks the timer on the oven, another twenty minutes. Twenty minutes, twenty minutes, twenty minutes, twenty minutes. Without being aware of it she starts massaging her hands, as if they could not bear to be left to their own devices, with nothing to do. Anita is aware of these times when she is no longer a light, delicate, competent woman. She feels as heavy as a watermelon, as clumsy as a crude wooden doll. Everything around her takes on a bloated and ungainly aspect. Her breathing is a roar in her chest, her heartbeats are strokes of a gong, the ticking of the timer fills the kitchen with its clamor. Anita claps her hands, once, twice, in an attempt to extricate herself from this odd hypnotic state, but that does not work. She makes haste to go up to the second floor and there, on the threshold of Laura's bedroom, *hey presto*, she recovers her composure, her poise.

The room is primrose yellow. On the floor a carpet, toys, a chest against the wall. There is also a wardrobe, and a big giraffe woven from knotted straw. At the center of the room a magnificent child's bed made of wood, painted in soft yellow, the palest that exists. Laura is asleep, her arms raised above her head. This bedroom is Adam's creation—apart from the toys, he has made everything. Anita sits right down on the floor and inhales the innocence and calm that this room gives off.

A few minutes later she hears the timer on the oven. And at the same moment her child wakes up. And Anita once more becomes that light, competent woman, the woman who feeds, washes, cleans, sweeps, polishes, shines, tidies, cooks, laughs, provokes laughter, plays, gardens, shops, loves her husband, her daughter, her house.

Nobody asked her to become this woman. Her husband, her dear Adam, always seems satisfied—with what he has on his plate; with the way she looks after their daughter; with the arrangement of the flowers in the vase; with what she grants him when they are intimate together. Deep inside her there is, as it were, a little pocket of emptiness, and when she gets up in the morning, this pocket whistles, as do cavities hollowed out of rocks. And then she spends her time eager to fill this space. Each task accomplished to the full (all the housework, potato puree made by hand, the books in alphabetical order, each nursery rhyme) brings her closer to the feeling of being complete—being completely a woman, completely a mother, completely a wife. She can no longer turn her back on the reality, the weight and volume of her life. Her daughter = 28 pounds; her house = 30 by 36 feet floor area; the number of diapers used daily = 7; the number of potatoes for a puree = 2; the number of measures of powdered milk needed for a five-ounce baby bottle = 5; the correct temperature for a drink = 82 degrees Fahrenheit; the furrows between her eyebrows = 1; white hairs above her right ear = 3; the income she brings in each month = 0; the hours in her day = 24.

Sometimes Anita has the feeling she is tirelessly reliving the same day, but she does not seek to make any changes at all, on the contrary, she catches herself wanting to do exactly the same thing at the same time, bath, meal, housework, games, taking a walk, looking, listening. Perhaps through this repetition she will finally discover what it is that eludes her, recover what she has lost (but what was it?), find the solution (but to what problem?) or the answer (but to what question?).

At night she wakes up, goes up to the attic, and opens old cardboard boxes. What she finds there is notebooks, poems, articles she wrote when she was on her internship, countless ideas for novels; she rereads the letters her parents sent her when she was a student. She studies everything attentively and absorbs her own dreams, her own desires, her own fantasies, so as not to lose touch completely with that other Anita, the one who wanted a career out in the world, the one who wanted to write a novel.

Occasionally she has enough energy left to open a notebook. Then she writes about her daily life, the birthday, the well-laid table, the cake, her child's downy skin, the incredible elasticity of the hours of the day . . . On occasion something mysterious arises out of her words, something almost as palpable as a caress, and then she finds this new path she is following has some meaning, far away from her former dreams. Then Anita becomes convinced that this new life is no less courageous than that other one out in the world with its bus journeys, nannies, and day cares. No, her life is no less honorable than that other one amid the world's noise, a life of listening, talking, thinking, writing.

A man who paints

NIGHT HAS FALLEN ON THE FOREST, THE HOUSE BREATHES SOFTLY like a great animal in a deep sleep. Adam is washing the dishes. On the table lie newspapers, mail, papers of various kinds, a doll, a teddy bear, a bunch of keys. Two felt pens without their caps. Faded peonies stand in brownish water that gives off a smell of sickly sweet decay, their petals scattered around the vase.

He hears Anita coming downstairs but does not turn around. She opens the refrigerator. She is muttering. *I had to read three stories. The comfort blanket had got lost. I've left the light on.*

Adam clenches his teeth. Every day it's the same old story. Every day the house is in chaos. He turns off the tap and looks out through the bay windows, but they are too dirty for him to be able to catch a glimpse of anything at all. When did things change here, in this house? Whatever became of that sweet and comfortable feeling of the first years? His wife and child safe and warm in the house he had built while he himself was out in the world. He would come home in the evening and something would be simmering on the stove, there would be a partly eaten cake under a glass cover on the table, he would hear laughter in the well-ordered living room. In the evening his wife would talk to him and listen to him, admiring and loving. In those days words flowed like honey. Was that a dream?

"What are you doing, Anita?"

"There was a piece of cheesecake in the fridge."

"I just threw it away."

"You did?"

"It was a week old, Anita. Could you put the plates away, please? Or clear the table? Or throw out those goddamned flowers?"

"Hey, take it easy. I'm just going to eat a yogurt and then I'll do it."

Adam turns around and for a fraction of a second he feels he is in the presence of a stranger. What has become of his wife with her long hair and shining eyes, her long colorful skirts and her scent of vanilla? The woman leaning nonchalantly against the door of the fridge is thin and dressed in faded, limp clothes. Although there is so much to be done in this house she is slowly consuming a yogurt while eyeing him furtively as if she were a teenager. But she is no longer a teenager, she has a daughter, she has a husband, she has a house, she has a home, and she cannot make do with a yogurt for supper!

"Anita, how long is it since we last sat down to a proper meal together? Have you seen yourself? You're all skin and bone. Do you eat any lunch on your daily tours of the countryside?"

"Yes, I eat lunch."

"Who are you kidding? How much longer is this going to go on?"

"What? How much longer is what going to go on? Precisely what are you talking about?"

Anita's question disconcerts him for a moment. Precisely what is he talking about? Is it really all about her losing weight, about meals not eaten together, about dishes to be washed and windows to be cleaned? What is it about his wife that irritates him so much?

"Do you think I'm wasting my time, is that it? You'd like me to stay home, like a good little girl, cook the meals, do the housework, and spend my time waiting for you, looking after the house. Oh my, there's such a lot to do here. Oh my, this lovely house! Oh my, this lovely prison!"

"Anita!!"

Adam smashes a plate against the edge of the sink. It breaks with a dull, sly noise, like their argument. He had hoped for something a little more theatrical, but, even so, Anita is surprised. He points a piece of the broken plate at her and then makes sweeping gestures with this fragment of white Limoges porcelain, the Taj Mahal series, a wedding present.

"How can you say that? How can you think that I want to keep you locked up, that I want to turn you into a—what—into a mere stay-at-home mother? That's what you're insinuating, isn't it?"

"I don't know, I don't know anymore." Anita clasps both hands to her head, as if seeking to rearrange and concentrate her thoughts. She senses that this is a battle lost in advance. And yet when she is in her car, bowling along the country lanes, she knows exactly what is in her mind, what she wants, what she longs for. But here, in their house, facing her husband, the words elude her, the sounds are out of sync, her sentences feeble. Now her immigrant's nervousness comes to the surface, her doubts about language, her hesitations in thought. In the old days, when they were in Paris, Adam used to experience the same hesitations, the same fleeting, nervous feelings, but he has forgotten them. He has forgotten that he was once regarded as a typical provincial, while she is still seen as a typical foreigner.

"I don't understand. You've become obsessed by this region. You're doing research on the game of pétanque, for God's sake!"

"But I have to prove myself."

"Oh no, for pity's sake! Spare me all that. It was for a match between two clubs and for a piece you were not even allowed to sign! I thought you wanted to write books, novels. You were always talking about it. You wanted to be a journalist. You wanted to write proper articles, didn't you? Is that what these are, proper articles?"

Anita stares at him, her hands clasping her head again, looking completely lost. Adam lowers his voice a little, takes a step toward Anita. This is the moment for him to strike home with all the things he has already said before: give up this dead-end job, these days spent plowing back and forth across the countryside, these pieces buried in the middle of the paper. It is the moment to make her understand that she must come back home, become his wife again and the mother of their child. Adam would like her to grasp the extent to which he is, in point of fact, a modern man. He is offering her time and freedom, for heaven's sake! She has no need to work. She could write, she could read, she could leave to him the trouble of getting his hands dirty out in the world.

Anita is silent because she feels certain Adam would not understand what she might manage to say. This man standing before her, her husband, has lived here on this terrain since his birth, he knows the trees, he knows the highways and byways. His local knowledge matches his own memories. He is not trying to be a different person, he is not trying to make people forget the color of his skin, his accent. When he gets up in the morning and looks at the pine forest, no images of the tangled masses of banyan trees come to his mind. Adam would not understand the efforts she makes each day to finally belong here, so that, in the end, words (in articles, in short stories, in a novel) may take her place and speak for her. That evening Anita feels very remote from her husband. That evening she is a stranger in her own house.

Encouraged by Anita's silence, Adam continues. He warms to the topic, feels proud, hears himself as he speaks. This evening he is finally going to convince her. He takes another step forward.

"Those people are exploiting you. They send you out scouring the countryside. You take all the pictures yourself. You write your stories. You hand them in neatly and tidily. They've no grounds for complaint about you, that's for sure. They pay you peanuts and you're happy with that, you sign up for more. You're due to meet the editor tomorrow, aren't you? What are the odds that he'll say there's nothing for you at the moment, but he's well pleased with your work? He'll hold that carrot out to you forever, Anita. You're worth so much more than that."

Adam is very close to his wife now. All it takes is for him to lean toward her a little and with an almost imperceptible rustling, a fluttering of wings, she falls into his arms and he gathers her up. He would like to tell her how much he truly misses her. Her bracelets, her hair that becomes curly in summer, her soft brown skin, her long skirts that finish up with dirty hems by the end of the day, her wooden bead necklaces that reach down to her navel, the untidy bunches of wildflowers she used to scatter throughout the house, her passionate outbursts of high praise for some piece of prose or verse, the way she quickly grew heated about some conflict, some idea, some topic, the idiosyncratic way she had of carrying Laura on one hip, with a hand tucked under her buttocks, as if this were all perfectly normal, this conjoined being growing out of her hip, the stillness of her body when she is making notes in her gray binder, her vanilla scent.

"Okay, Adam. If the editor doesn't offer me anything tomorrow, I'll quit."

Adam hugs her tighter still, the way she likes to be hugged, and lifts her into the air.

Later Adam wakes up, with the hairs all over his body standing on end. He cocks an ear but all that reaches him is Anita breathing deeply beside him. He turns his head toward her and the contours of her body beneath the cover seem to him quite angular, as if gathered up in a little heap, and that makes him think of the carcasses of famished dogs. The vision only lasts for a moment but it makes him feel quite uneasy. He does not like thinking about his wife's body as a little heap, he does not want his wife's pinched body to remind him of dead dogs. He squeezes close to her. She stirs, murmurs something. Her warm breath, amazingly sweet, as if she fed only on milk, lingers over Adam's face and he feels better. He strokes her brow, following her hairline. He closes his eyes.

Ideas and images dance gently behind his eyelids: the meeting at 10:00 a.m. at the town hall to present the plans for the new gymnasium, Laura's red boots in the trunk of the car, Anita's black bra hanging from the bathroom door handle . . .

Then he sees Anita standing upright in her study, lost in thought, reflecting as if within herself. When had he seen her like this? Yesterday, last week, three months ago? The more the image imposes itself on him the more Anita seems to be disappearing amid the yellow light spilling into the room, crossing it, engulfing it, swallowing it. This light becomes dense, a yellow shot through with orange that dazzles everything, a rippling sunlight blotting out all traces, all shadows, all presences.

How to capture this color, this density, this impression of movement that is both slow and elastic?

Adam gets up, fully alert. He walks along the passage, glances in at Laura, goes downstairs, opens the door, crosses the garden. The wet grass attaches little drops to the bottom of his pajama pants. He goes into the wooden hut at the edge of the forest.

Within a few years this space, which is as big as their tiny apartment in Paris, has become what artists like to call a studio. Adam does not yet dare to use this term, there are a good many words like this that he keeps at arm's length and is wary of when they come trippingly to the tongue: *artist, inspiration, happiness, unhappiness.* When he was a little boy his father used to say of him *Adam likes painting* and this phrase, one that evokes charming things, equipment kept in a jar, a well-ordered work table, would suit him very well these days. Even if his material (pots of paint, pigment oils, turpentine, brushes, hammers, pincers, thumbtacks, oiled canvases, rags) now occupies one whole wall of his studio, even if his worktable is here, there, and everywhere (the walls, odd corners, the floor), even if *charming* would not be the adjective that would spring to mind in someone seeing these pictures, Adam still likes to think of himself as "a man who paints."

In his studio Adam remains seated on a stool for a while, staring into the center of the room. He is concentrating on the image that made him leave the warmth of his bed. For some time now he has felt the urge to paint in a different way—forget faces, landscapes, detail, he would like to work with simpler, more authentic subject matter but he does not know how to do it, where to begin. He lacks something, but what?

The truth is it does not matter very much. Adam is thirty-five. Unaware of the cruel way time chips away at things, he is not affected by reality. He is here and now. He draws. He paints. He makes things. He imagines. He designs. He sands and polishes. He works at his art, at what he is creating, without asking himself questions, without a mountain to climb, without a jungle to cross, without any obstacles. Moments before he had been that disgruntled husband, falling out with his wife, breaking a plate, arguing with her. Moments before, too, he had been that man seeking the warmth of a desired body, the comfort of being loved and desired in return. Now all he is is this man preparing a canvas, mixing pigments with linseed oil. He is nothing more than his painting and his painting is his alone. He is without fear, without guilt, without a path to follow, no meals to prepare, no laundry to hang, no shopping to do, no child to amuse. There is nobody whom he has to convince of his right to be where he is, with no sound in his ears, no sunlight coming in to interrupt his train of thought. He is creation itself.

"The song of the fourth floor"

ANITA ARRIVES IN THE CITY AT 11:00 IN THE MORNING. IT IS THE day after her quarrel with Adam. She parks her car behind the church, walks briskly across the paved square with its abundant flowers, passes through the shopping mall that she uses as a shortcut, emerges into another square where the surface resembles the ones used in children's playgrounds, and goes into the building on the left. It is an ordinary four-story building where the second, third, and fourth floors each have balconies that come to a point and remind her of a kind of vertebral column (she must remember to ask Adam if there are such styles in architecture as "pointed," "round," "semicircular," "pierced"). On the first floor of the building there are fascinating machines that produce offset plates, as well as scanners, harsh lights, dark corners, and men with mustaches and fierce eyes, raising their voices above the *boom, boom, boom* of the rotary presses. The second floor houses the newspaper's reception office, the secretarial and administrative staff, the archives, the cafeteria. On the third floor are the proofreaders, the editorial secretaries, the layout artists, the graphics team, and the pasteup artists.

On the fourth floor, where she stops, is the reporters' room. Facing the door to this is the glass cage of the editor, Christian Voubert, a very tall, very slender man who, when he rises from his chair, unwinds like a liana. She is due to meet him this morning.

On either side of the cage the L-shaped work spaces are arranged in pairs. They might seem identical: beige computer, black keyboard, pencil holder, stacks of gray wire filing trays, telephone. But personal impulses have turned each space into a little home away from home: a photograph, a pebble, a bunch of dried flowers, a chipped cup, a piece of origami, an indescribable clutter, a quotation.

Anita breathes in and opens the door and would love to be able to capture a snatch of this soundtrack and edit it into her own personal, intimate, and subjective compilation of the best sounds in the world.

This fragment she would call "the song of the fourth floor": the clatter of a keyboard, an animated conversation about how many words a report on the previous day's rugby match might be worth, the noise of the fax machine, a telephone ringing, pages being turned, the coffee machine spluttering, the muffled sound of a television, laughter, greetings. And this fragment would have smells to go with it: those of coffee, paper, the sea air blowing in at the windows, that of ink.

Anita has no desk here, far from it, because a year ago Christian Voubert told her that the only thing he could offer her *for the moment* was work as a "stringer" (the moment in question not being one as in the dictionary definition *a brief period of time*, but on the contrary, one synonymous with *for the foreseeable future*). Anita had then learned that *stringer* is a term used on regional newspapers for the freelance journalists who fill up the pages of local news, that is to say, half the paper. Brief stories with photographs and the feel-good atmosphere of weekends with the family. It was not what she had hoped for but there was this business of *for the moment*, and there was also the business of proving herself.

Over a year ago on the same floor, in the same glass office, Christian Voubert sees Anita for the first time after she has submitted a spontaneous job application.

"This is a difficult time, and, well, you know, looking at you, now, I don't know if you can write."

"I've already published articles in *Claire* magazine. I sent them with my résumé."

"Yes, yes, agreed. But, how can I put it? This is a daily newspaper, not a women's magazine. And you don't come from around here, do you?"

"No."

"You see, that's what I'm saying. Now, to be a stringer is to know the region. To go out and meet people. To take the pulse of the countryside, eat pork for breakfast and drink wine at ten in the morning. To be like doctors in the old days, you know . . ."

Christian Voubert had sighed deeply as he gave her the bad news. *(We don't need anyone else at the moment, but I will not hesitate to contact you should the occasion arise.)*

Anita was watching him closely and was reminded of her father's deep inhalations and exhalations when he was embarking on his daily yoga session. A big veranda, bougainvilleas, a lean dog with half-closed eyes, the dawn, a man doing his *vipassana* meditation, birds calling to one another in the trees, strange how memories creep in where nothing calls them forth.

Did she give him a faint smile, there in that glass office? Did she relax a little? Did a hint of something touching and sincere appear in her face that caused a sudden shift in Christian Voubert's resolve?

"Anita, it's your lucky day. We're going to give you a few months' trial. Agreed? You'll be a stringer. That's all I can offer you for the moment. Later on, we'll see. You'll have to prove yourself."

That evening, standing on a chair in front of Adam, with a rug draped around her like a toga, Anita had declaimed:

Friends, Romans, countrymen, lend me your ears
To be a stringer is to know the region
To be a stringer is to take the pulse of the countryside

*Monsieur Voubert, my friends, tells us to eat pork for breakfast
and drink wine in the morning
And Monsieur Voubert is an honorable man . . .*

Adam had laughed until the tears came to his eyes.

Anita was making a joke of it but she was too naive, too happy
to read between the lines, to guess at Christian Voubert's private
thoughts as he wondered how long *a woman like that* would stick
at it with that job.

A woman like that was the sum total of prejudices, clichés, and
impressions he had formed in his mind as a result of his meeting
with Anita.

A foreigner: she doesn't know her way around and makes mistakes in French.

A young mother: not always available and gets depressed.

Married to an architect whose office is three streets away from
the newspaper: a housewife looking for an occupation so as not
to get even more depressed.

Has lived in Paris: arrogant.

Native of an island: lazy.

But as Christian Voubert will discover, Anita is not *a woman
like that*. She calls at the editorial office every Monday. The schedule for the day is posted at 10:00 a.m. and she comes in through
the door at 10:07. The top lines on the schedule are devoted to the
news stories that will occupy the front and back pages in the paper.
Politics, social news, financial news, news in brief, environmen-
tal topics, culture. She reads through the topics, the names of the
reporters, occasionally there is a note of the style of coverage or
the angle the article will take.

Lower down on the schedule there is a list of locales, with a
note of the commune, the topic, the name of the stringer. There
is never any note of the angle or the style. Anita looks through
the topics to which no stringer has been assigned and every week
she writes down a minimum of two and a maximum of five. She
naturally has her own criteria—she only covers events that take

place between 9:30 a.m. and 3:00 p.m., so she can drop Laura off at school and pick her up; she never works on Wednesdays because Laura is at home then; she notes down all the events happening on the weekend because that is when Adam takes over for her at home. Next she makes her way to Claire, the news editor. She is a good-natured, plump woman who talks fast and gives good advice. She is forever tossing her head backward to rearrange her pretty curls, which seem to be mounted on springs. A coquettish gesture on the verge of becoming a nervous tic, thinks Anita. Claire confirms the topics or not, decides which days the stories will appear, and Anita can begin the week.

She accepts whatever falls to her equally calmly and seriously: the final interclub match between pétanque teams, a veterans' reunion, the annual bazaar at a primary school, a miniconcert given by a Johnny Hallyday lookalike at an old people's home, a performance of *Antigone* by a high school dramatic society, a day of regional cuisine, the deliberations of the jury for a "Houses in Bloom" competition.

On her first time out, in a village where they were celebrating the birthday of a pair of ninety-year-old twins, she had failed to understand the looks she attracted, both surprised and questioning. People responded to her politely but warily. She had great difficulty in getting them to tell her stories about the two spinster ladies who had been born in this very village. The best she got was the grocer's son telling her how they used to wash one another's feet each morning. Twice the mayor asked her if she was indeed the person he had spoken to on the telephone the previous day and for how long she would be standing in for Georges (the regular stringer who was down with flu). She did not manage to take good group photographs, people kept drifting away as fast as they gathered. All she managed to take was a picture of the ninety-year-old ladies in profile, after they had blown out their candles, their faces swathed in a faint mist. Nobody offered her a piece of cake.

There Anita was, all too visible, and yet appallingly invisible. She had reread her notes and reckoned that she would have enough to write two hundred and fifty words. She walked around the village, several small boys were playing a game of tag. Stone houses, lace curtains, spick and span alleyways, what are the lives of people here? What are they thinking about, those young men leaning against the wall of the town hall, their mopeds within easy reach, watching the celebration without taking part, with a mixture of scorn and derision in their eyes? She took several extra photographs, picked up a black pebble streaked with mauve, gathered a few daisies from the roadside for Laura.

When she got back to her car she caught her reflection in the window and suddenly she understood. She was not at all the person they had been expecting. The game she sometimes played with Laura came to mind: spot the odd one out. A vegetable among fruits, a pair of spectacles among pairs of shoes, a red flower in a yellow field. She was the stranger with dark skin (what to call it? black? brown?) among the whites.

Anita got into her car but did not drive off right away. She had certainly found it difficult doing her work that day but she could not set aside the feeling of pure joy that had overcome her as she noted a few lines on her pad and the words had come to her naturally, authentically. She had felt capable of being in the moment while at the same time observing it. That instant in this village forgotten by the tourist routes was one of absolute truth. These winding lanes, which had followed the same course for hundreds of years, these stones, gleaming from being trodden underfoot, what do they tell and what effect do they have on people? Was this not just what she had wanted to do for so many years? To chronicle the ins and outs of the world? She could not give up so soon.

To be sure, this was not the way she had imagined the profession. She remembered the editorial offices in Paris where she had done an internship and the somewhat unreal aspects of it that she had not particularly enjoyed at the time, but that, in the end, she occasionally missed a little, those extremely elegant and well shod young women who chose to call themselves "girls," the assignations kept amid the hubbub of the city, the apartments smelling of coffee and beeswax, evenings spent quietly writing her article, in her studio apartment, in a café, anywhere at all, it did not matter, provided one was in Paris.

She started her car and began composing her piece in her mind. There was no question of giving up so soon.

Week in, week out, she deposits Laura at the school and plows back and forth across the countryside. On the first few occasions she braces herself fully for the moment when she must call up all her energy, as one calls up the sum total of a lifetime's experience to fashion a shield from it, the moment when looks will be focused on her. Every time there is the same surprise, the same questioning, whatever the location—a village square, an athletic field, a forest road, a cultural and sports center, a school playground. She would like to be able to spare them this but apparently on the telephone she has no accent, her name does not suggest anything foreign, and when the conversation has gone well and ends with the words "See you tomorrow; we'll be waiting for you!" she would love to be able to warn them—the way you warn people that your child is allergic to nuts or your elderly father is a bit deaf—but the truth is, this is not the same. Being allergic to nuts does not show on your face.

When she gets out of the car and closes the door she cannot refrain from glancing at her reflection in the window and remembering who she is, so as not to forget the image she presents to other people. To act as if everything were normal, not be offended, not be angry, never to jump to conclusions.

Week in, week out, she throws back her shoulders, smiles, steps out confidently but without vanity. She dresses in a neutral style, leaving her colored bracelets, her skirts with mirrors, her brightly colored dresses, and her wooden necklaces at home.

Gradually, it seems to her that the looks of surprise are less frequent. Occasionally someone will ask her a question and get into conversation with her. Occasionally someone will ask her opinion, someone will let drop that they liked her last piece, someone will take her arm, someone will invite her to taste something, someone will insist on her drinking a cup of coffee, someone will ask if she is married, if she has children.

Then on the journey home the beauty of the countryside seeps into her, the poppies, the colza, the forsythia beside the roads, the colors floating above the meadows like a motley kite, the vibrant heat at the edges of the fields of corn, the cool emanating from the pine forests.

Now she is not weary, not vulnerable, she believes in the possibility of being an equal, a fellow human being, a sister, even. Now that deep inner thrill returns to her, the slow reawakening of that blazing hope of her youth, that of becoming a writer. Now in the evening she takes up a notebook again, she begins to write, to hope, but each time, as in a soufflé, the words collapse. But this is not a problem, for she is convinced that soon she will find a story to tell, a fantastic idea that will stand up, that will stay the course. A story she can keep an eye on from afar, even when tired, even when weary, even when disappointed, and it will be like a constant light. Yes, a story, a good story to tell.

Month after month, without fail, she delivers her pieces on time, without mistakes, headline and copy in place. Still nothing to report, says Claire. She comes to Christian Voubert's attention because in an account of the annual reunion of veteran soldiers in a mountain village there is a word that he had never come across in French in his life before and that he had looked up in the dictionary: "Like a *griot*, Sylvain H. rose to his feet. Strumming on his guitar, he softly sang the old Resistance song: *Le Chant des Partisans.*"

Griot: traveling poet and musician in black Africa, repository of the oral culture, said to be in communication with spirits.

The editor had been moved by this sentence, as if he, too, had been there at this village, where, as Anita had written, the women wear "blouses decorated with flowers that never fade," as if he, too, had heard the song. And for the first time in many years he had thought about his own father.

And he told himself that Anita was not a woman like the rest . . . By degrees, with the passage of these trial months, all the faults he had imputed to her were disappearing. The very same causes resulted in different effects, different clichés, different empty phrases.

Foreigner: a fresh eye on the region, relish for the French language.

Young mother: a welcome sensitivity.

Married to an architect whose office is just around the corner from the town hall: a woman attentive to the aesthetics of the region.

Having lived in Paris: experience.

Native of a remote island: sensitive to the region's own strong identity.

A year or more had passed. Christian Voubert had decided that she had proved herself.

That Tuesday, when Anita walks into his office at 11:17, Christian Voubert tells himself that something about her has changed, but he cannot put his finger on it. She looks him straight in the eye.

"So, how's it going out in the territory, Anita?"

"It's going well. Everything's going well."

"Yes, I think everything's going very well indeed. Yours is not obviously the work of a stringer. I've had several phone calls from people pleased with your work. I like getting phone calls like that."

Anita remains silent, her hands resting on her knees. She is thinking back to her argument with Adam the night before. Now that Christian Voubert has congratulated her on her work he will tell her he has nothing to offer her, *for the moment.*

"Good. Now, Anita, this Friday there's a cultural evening with music from the island of Réunion and a concert by a singer of, hang on . . . ma . . . something."

"Maloya?"

"Yes, that's it. I've never heard of it. They want to add this music into the UNESCO cultural heritage program and I thought that, as you come from that neck of the woods . . . It's quite close by, isn't it, Mauritius?"

"Yes, it's very close."

"There you are. I thought you could do an article for the arts page on Saturday. You'd do a long piece, let's say nine hundred and fifty words in total, about this traditional music. What it is. The history of the thing, its development, and how it's part of the French cultural heritage, all that. We need two separate sections, one on the concert itself, perhaps a picture of the singer, I can't remember his name, and another on the business of adding this music into the cultural heritage. How does that strike you?"

"It's an excellent idea."

"Good, but take care, Anita. The account of the concert has to be written the same night. You'll have an hour, an hour and a half at the very most, to do it. Do you think you can manage that? Yes? Very good. Claire will give you the details better than I can. If it goes well, you'll have other opportunities like this. Does that suit you?"

"Yes, Monsieur Voubert. Thank you."

"Good. You can call me Christian."

For the first time since she walked into the office she smiles at him (something that lights up her soft face and makes her eyes shine) and Christian Voubert has to restrain himself from coming around his desk to throw his arms about her.

As she is leaving he realizes that she is no longer wearing on her wrists those colored bracelets that tinkled gently as she moved. A pity. They suited her well.

Anita does what she generally does: she selects three topics from the board, discusses them with Claire, drinks a coffee and consults the archives. Once outside she begins running toward the beach, laughing. She feels as if her joy were trailing a great glittering train behind her and that this could carry the whole town with it: that young woman in a long skirt drinking coffee on a café terrace, that man in a gray jacket walking briskly along, the old lady in sneakers pulling her shopping cart, the girl in a tight-fitting dress smoking in front of her swimsuit store, the ice cream man in his striped jersey sitting on his stool, the balloons all ready, waiting for the children, the carousel, at a standstill, surrounded by a protective net, the people strolling on the prome-nade, the old men on the benches, the dogs, the cats at windows, the profusion of plants with mauve flowers all along the coast road, that strip of sand, the azure blue sea, the spring sky.

Later, stretched out on the sand, her eyes closed, her heart now beating regularly, she begins to dream about next Saturday, when Adam collects the newspaper after his run. He will be bathed in sweat, he will come leaping upstairs four steps at a time. Despite their quarrel, despite all he had said to her, predicted, advised, this first article will please him. Yes, he will say, you were right to persevere. They will be happy. They will be proud. They will feel filled with the courage and energy they need to live this life of theirs. It will be the renewal they were hoping for.

Today

IT IS 7:00 A.M. THE MORNING IS HERE, SIDLING INTO EVERY NOOK AND cranny in the house, proclaiming this day in all its cruel density and reality. Anita swallows a vial of royal jelly and avoids looking at her reflection in the bay windows. She must not flinch today. She is so afraid of this day, she dreads every step she will take, every word she will utter, she dreads her daughter waking up, she is afraid of taking her husband in her arms, she is afraid of what they can say to one another. These days Anita is afraid of everything. A few years ago she believed she and Adam had a destiny. This was neither vanity nor arrogance but the quiet certainty that they were, in their own way, exceptional. Where did it come from, this conviction that together they would achieve something unique?

Anita remembers with a twinge of embarrassment that on occasion she pictured an article about the two of them in a very smart magazine along the lines of *Architectural Digest*. She would have written a great novel that attracted notable coverage; he would have painted pictures of great beauty, designed a striking modern building; they would arrange visits to their fine timber house, the study, the studio, the extensive bookshelves, they would pose beside the lilac tree with the forest visible behind them. They would be witty, mysterious, intelligent, generous, humble, and respectful and insist that their daughter's face be pixelated.

Anita had been convinced that someday they would step into the limelight, they would be discovered, as a perfect diamond is suddenly discovered in a mine explored a thousand times before, a remarkable manuscript in a trunk in an attic, or a painting by an old master hidden beneath a layer of dirt. One little thing would suffice, so she surmised, to catapult them into something extraordinary, into what she called *a destiny*.

That "little thing" was Adèle.

"Maman? Maman!"

Anita is snatched out of her reverie, hurries through the living room without looking at the mist rising off the forest, ignoring Adam's triptych that still hangs over the fireplace. As she reaches the threshold of the bedroom she straightens her back, tenses like a bow, smiles broadly and her jaw makes a little clicking sound. She goes in.

Laura is sitting on her bed, her face set in an expression of surprise and fear. She is almost thirteen, her once curly hair is smooth now. Her eyes are slightly slanted. Sometimes, when her movements and words are measured, she has the elegant look of an Asian woman. Laura eyes her mother, then the wheelchair near the door, then her mother again. She grasps the bars that are raised on both sides of the bed.

"Maman? What's happening? Where's my bed?"

On some days Laura's memory is disturbingly sharp: she remembers the hoarfrost on the ferns, her pink coat, Adèle on the jetty at the lake, she recalls waking up in the hospital and all that she has lost. Those are difficult days. She is upset, furious, desperate, refuses her medicines, loathes her life, her mother, her father. At other times, as today, she thinks she is still eight years old, she does not know that her father is in prison and that Adèle is no more. She believes she can climb trees, run about in the garden, go to school.

Anita goes up to her, slides the bar down, slips in beside her daughter.

"It's only a bad dream, *ma chérie*. Go back to sleep for a little while, it's still early."

"Will you stay with me, *Maman*?"

"Yes, of course, *ma chérie*."

Adèle often used to sleep in this room. A few of the things she loved are still there: the pretty turquoise box on the bedside table, the lamp mounted on driftwood, the faded postcards of the region in frames the color of old gold. She used to say to Anita that this house was as warm as a mother's embrace. She told Anita that here she could forget her past life.

Anita chokes back her tears. She presses close to Laura. If only she could borrow a little of her amnesia from her this morning. It would be so good for the space of a few hours, to forget those four years, five months, and thirteen days. It would be so wonderful still to believe in that destiny of hers.

PART TWO

The day of the grass snake

ON THE MORNING OF HER MEETING WITH ANITA, ADÈLE CATCHES sight of a grass snake behind the bus shelter. She spends a good while observing this long creature, which is yellower than she would have expected, the way it slithers very slowly toward the fallow land nearby, and the stirring of the vegetation as it moves along. She cocks her head on one side, intrigued by the presence of this reptile, as if it were an animal from another era, not quite prehistoric, but from the days of her childhood (she calls to mind the columns of ants she used to like watching in the backyard). She remembers her mother used to say that a grass snake was a portent of change, but Adèle has long since ceased to believe in such things.

They are all there at the bus stop, the daylight phantoms, more or less the same as those she has been coming across there for quite a few years. (Adèle does not count, she says a few, quite a few, a long time, not such a long time, many, not many, a few, very few.) She does not remember faces but she recognizes the look of things, habits, sounds, smells, gestures: the blue smoke from a cigarette being shared by the young people gathered at the back of the bus shelter, the sound of tapping on a packet of Tic Tac mints held in the palm (a rhythm of maracas), a ring finger applying balm to the lips, the cotton print skirts of women from Senegal, the brand names plastered across T-shirts, the white tracksuits, the black pants made shiny by frequent ironing, the

Nigerian women's brightly colored scarves, the Jamaican caps, the electric-blue mascara, the eyeliner in the style of the singer, Barbara, the sandalwood-based beauty masks of the women from the Comoros Islands, the *tsiit, tsiit, tsiit* of the personal stereos, the slim-line dance shoes, the cork platform shoes, the sneakers with huge tongues.

When the bus arrives Adèle looks around but the snake has vanished. Something tiny subsides within her. Then she gets onto the bus and forgets all about the grass snake and portents, good or bad. She prepares herself for the long day ahead, thinking about it, as she has thought about many things for years now, without any particular emotion. A day is made up of a series of tasks to be performed, each within an amount of time allotted in advance, each at a more or less specified hour, the completion of one activity signaling the start of another and so on.

From Monday to Friday she catches the 7:00 bus to go and work for the Lesparet family. She begins her assignment at 7:45 by clearing the breakfast table while Madame Lesparet buzzes around her, a stream of words spilling out of her mouth (Cecilia Lesparet calls this the morning debriefing). Adèle listens attentively and stores these words away in a corner of her brain. Cecilia Lesparet is a slim woman of thirty-eight with fair, straight hair trimmed to precisely one-tenth of an inch below the lobes of both ears, which are pierced and ornamented with two Tahiti pearl stub earrings. She is a management consultant, as her business card specifies. So, the debriefing. How the children were the previous evening and during the night, together with diverse and varied instructions that are prefaced by "may I venture to remind you that," but Adèle does not hold it against her. Cecilia Lesparet is always correct, she pays her on the fifth day of every month, cash in a fresh, sealed envelope, she occasionally adds a few restaurant coupons, she puts clothes she no longer wants aside for her, unfashionable handbags, half-used bottles of perfume. Cecilia never asks her questions about her private life, how

she spends her spare time. It should also be mentioned that sur-
veillance cameras in the house record the smallest of her actions.

At 8:15 Adèle goes back out of the house to walk the children
to school (two to a nursery school, one to the primary school)
and less than half an hour later she returns to a big empty house.
This could be daunting, the silence, the untidiness, all the things
she has to do, all the vacuousness and pointlessness of a strange
house, but Adèle does not consider matters in broad terms, in
terms of the whole picture, in generalities, making a link between this vast house and her vast loneliness. No, she thinks
about the tasks to be performed and this is how her day passes,
without mishap, without distress, without bitterness. And once
you think about a day like this, the thing is, there's just so much
to do. She is kind and gentle with the children, she makes well-
balanced meals for them, plays with them a lot and on the way
back from school, where there are no cameras, she treats them
to candy and sodas. At 6:45 Monsieur Lesparet comes home.
When Adèle hears the gates opening and the crunch of the gravel
beneath the wheels of his elegant gray car, she checks off a list
of things in her head: meal prepared, housework done, laundry
aired, laundry ironed, children showered and fed, any aches and
pains to be reported or not. To Pascal Lesparet's "All well, Adèle?"
she has been replying almost every day for several years: "All well,
monsieur." She hugs the children and occasionally, just occasionally, there is something inside her that shivers at this moment,
especially if the children hug her tightly, with both arms around
her neck and she feels as if she could run away with them hanging around her neck like a human necklace, but it is a transitory
feeling, a passing impulse.

From Friday to Sunday, starting at 9:00 p.m., Adèle works as
a barmaid at the Bar Tropical, in the city. On Friday evenings,
after kissing the children goodbye, she walks down into the
city center. She passes along clean streets, observes the private
houses, the camellias, the stone pines that she is particularly

fond of, the pretty blue tiles with the house numbers on them, the paved areas, the lawns, the gravel, the rough plaster on a wall, the arabesques of ivy. The seasons pass, the colors change, the light fades, the cold surrounds her, the wind buffets her, scaffolding is erected and dismantled, a wall is knocked down, a great tree falls, revealing broad roots finely wrought like lace, there is a certain woman in a sweater who watches her passing day after day with the same expression of astonishment, but Adèle goes on her way and enjoys this feeling of descending into the city, toward the sea, toward the limits of the land. By the time she sees the high gates of the big hotel the air is suffused with particles of salt, becomes denser with humidity. At 8:00 she eats supper in the city: either at McDonald's, or at a Chinese restaurant, just occasionally at a pizzeria. Adèle always orders the same thing (a standard meal, fries, a soda; a hundred grams of chicken cooked with basil, a hundred grams of rice, a soda; a pizza margherita, a soda). She is never flustered, never vexed, it is as if she were invisible and this is precisely how she wants to be, and it is precisely like this that she survives.

At the Tropical she works at the bar, single-handed for several hours at a stretch. Amid the noise, the music, the shouting, she is always the same and this never ceases to amaze Denis, the manager and owner. He recruited her on a sudden impulse, this tall girl, as muscular as a hammer thrower. Adèle was running a stall of produce from the West Indies at the street market, in high summer. She stood there with a length of madras cotton tied about her neck as a scarf, offering plates of "accra" fritters and slabs of bread spread with spicy vegetable relish. Despite her silence, her giant stature, her shaved head, there was a crowd. Denis had just been walked out on by his barman (what was it he yelled as he left? *I've had enough of working in your shitty club for a black man's pay* or was it *working in your black man's club for shitty pay?*). He had gone up to her stall and, as he chewed on his minuscule slab of bread and relish, had said: "How would you like to work for me?"

She had eyed him with a calm stare and he had felt embarrassed and sheepish. He began again in somewhat softer and more respectful tones.

"My name's Denis Anicet. I manage the Tropical, the club on the big beach. Do you know it? I'm looking for someone to work in the bar."

"To do what?"

"Serve the customers, make cocktails, that kind of thing."

"I don't know how to make cocktails."

"No problem. We'll teach you. It's from Friday through Sunday. We open at nine and close at two."

"How do you pay?"

Not how much but *how*. That had not escaped Denis's attention but her dense, earthy, dark-brown gaze kept him from crowing.

"However you like. By check, by bank transfer, in cash."

"I prefer cash."

"No problem. Can you come and see me tomorrow?"

"Yes, at one p.m."

"Okay, then. See you tomorrow."

"I can make punch."

That was what she had said, or at least what he thought he had heard.

The next day she was waiting there in the parking lot, dressed in black, the same dark-brown eyes, the same shaved head. Denis had been struck and a little intimidated by her appearance. What a woman, he had thought.

So how long has Adèle been there now? Six years, maybe seven? Never any trouble, never one word louder than the next, never one word too many, either. All he had gathered was that she came from Mauritius and had no papers. But she seemed to be uncomplaining about this and the last thing Denis wanted was to get involved. At the bar she attracted a great crowd just

as she had on that stifling day in August. And, as she had said, or
not said, the punch she made would knock you flat.

Adèle always dresses in black, the only ornament she wears is
a fine silver wristband. She has a perfectly shaped cranium.

At closing time she leaves the bar gleaming (bar top, floor,
shelves, bottles, sink) and waits patiently for Denis at the entrance.
He drops her off outside the gates to the development where she
lives on the outskirts of the city. During the fifteen minutes it
takes to make this drive through a city now emptied of its inhabitants, sometimes it feels to them as if they were little motionless
figures in a glass bowl. Silence does not disturb Adèle and as time
has gone by Denis has learned to be equally appreciative of these
moments when time stands still. He no longer fidgets on his seat,
he no longer steals glances at her, no longer asks her questions.
When they reach the second traffic circle, the one dominated by
a structure in the form of an arrow, he slows down and drops her
close to the bus stop. He has never dared to walk with her up to
the front of her apartment building. He leaves the engine running
for two or three minutes, his ear cocked, his hand on the steering wheel, the car door locked—there are lots of stories about
certain districts in this suburb and at this time of night he has
no desire to invite trouble. Adèle walks around the bus shelter,
goes into the development, waves to him, and disappears. Denis
shifts into top gear and accelerates sharply, driven by the desire
to get back to his fine house, his garage with two car spaces, like
in American films, the lawn, and his wife's flowers that suddenly
seem so precious to him as he makes a U-turn to get onto the
bypass. He will go and kiss his children, take a shower, and later,
as he is quietly finishing off a cake, his face illuminated by the
light in the fridge door, he will wonder what Adèle's apartment
looks like.

Adèle's place: a space nine feet by twelve, a futon bed, an armchair, a table, a hot plate, a sink, a few cooking utensils, a chest of
drawers made of plywood, picked up one lucky day down at the

bottom of the apartment building. The toilets and bathroom are out in the corridor.

In her room: bare walls, every surface white and clean.

One has to picture her, this big woman just under six feet tall. Dressed in black, as always, coming into this room twelve feet by nine. She hangs up her bag, her jacket or her coat on the hook behind the door, takes off her shoes, puts on her Chinese slippers, things made of brightly colored satin, very comfortable but not durable. She makes her way with a slow tread over to the wash-basin and briskly soaps her hands and forearms before rinsing and drying them. When she comes back from the Lesparets' it will be barely 8:00 p.m. and she settles down in the armchair, her hands resting on her knees. She lets the sounds of the apartment building come to her, banging doors, mothers raising their voices, quarrels, television, laughter, footsteps above her, next door to her, and soon the world is nothing but a jumble of noise, exploding into white bubbles beneath her closed eyelids.

The evening passes, neither quickly nor slowly. She washes, eats, reads and cuts out odd news items from the papers, as if seeking to attract something that eludes her.

When she comes back from the club she goes to take a shower in the bathroom on the landing. Then she goes to bed, but whether at 10:30 or at 3:00 in the morning, sleep never comes soon enough.

All those years waiting for it to end. She had seen the start of the new century, magnificent fireworks over the sea, people hysterically happy, and she could not understand how she could still be there. It was not what she had foreseen when she sold her house, gave away her possessions, emptied her bank account. When she had gone into that dusty travel agent's office and paid for this trip to Europe. It was not what she had dreamed of when she shaved her head for the first time. Since she had not managed to die (oh, that inability to take her leave of life of her own accord!), she had thought she would disappear. She had read somewhere that thousands of people in the world vanish without a trace. So this was what she would do. Leave the land of her birth, take a train, then another, stop somewhere at a station at random, burn her papers, sleep in hotels, hang around, stop speaking, stop thinking, face up to strangers who don't look at you, expose herself to unfamiliar climates, spend or give away all her money, wander about, end up in the street, in a dark corner where no one will come looking for you, die, the way so many people die here—from cold, from hunger, from loneliness. Here, in Europe, death seemed to her more within reach, more silent.

But years later Adèle is still there. Sometimes she would like to reach down into herself with her hand and rummage about, the way fishermen rummage about in the innards of fish, to seize and root out the tiny spark, the tiny stubborn and vital spark, that causes her to survive, in spite of herself. What is it made of, this wretched thing, since she no longer has hope, or joy, or friends, or husband, or child?

In the end sleep overcomes her, a sleep full of dreams of days gone by (grass snakes, ants, husband, child, sunlight, typewriter). At dawn when nothing else remains behind her closed eyelids, she seems to see this little spark dancing. Then she gets up, as silently as the dust motes in the rays of the morning, and so she enters another day.

On that Friday, the morning of the day she will meet Anita, the grass snake is already far away, and the bus is particularly crowded. Adèle stands in the middle, facing the double doors. The young are gathered at the back, in a cluster, true to their gregarious instinct. Her right hand lightly grips the rail. The other is holding her bag slung over one shoulder. She gazes at the flattened, rather greasy hair of a young, highly scented woman who is sucking a Tic Tac mint. An old man is chewing the inside of his cheeks as he reads the free newspaper. There are two strollers close beside her and Adèle feels the weight of a little wheel on her foot. She does not stir. The children are fast asleep. There is a light ripple of talk from different parts of the vehicle and there, amid a mixture of smells, metal, damp wool, and sickly sweet perfume, she is thinking about the special event at the club this evening, a grand concert devoted to maloya, the traditional music of Réunion. Denis has asked her to make a dozen gallons of punch. She will have to get there earlier than usual, she will have no time for supper. She lets go of the rail to check that she has brought her cell phone.

Is there a sudden silence or has Adèle imagined it? As if something had sucked in all sounds, with the terrible sharp squeal of brakes suddenly applied. Adèle is hurled against the doors, which restrain her and throw her back onto the girl with the Tic Tac, then there is a great crash! She is flung against the doors once more. They burst open and Adèle comes flying out like a black eagle. She hears that voice, the one she knows well, saying *this is it, it's happening now*. But the feeling of being high up and floating does not last. She comes down onto something soft. She is not in pain, maybe she really is dead. She is on her back and the sky is so blue, so luminous, my God how beautiful it is! she says to herself. For the first time in half a lifetime she is using the words *God* and *beautiful* in the same sentence. She could reach out her hand and pluck down a scrap of sky. How would it taste? An airplane passes at that moment, floating, floating, it is a paper airplane, it is a perfect sky, the blue dotted with fleecy little clouds. There is a scent of earth, it has the good smell of childhood.

Adèle gets up on her elbows and everything becomes confused in her head. She recognizes this part of the suburbs, which is called Ville Nouvelle, with its meager, recently planted trees, the numerous traffic circles, the low walls in pastel shades surrounding the new residential areas, the newly tarred streets, and yet she has gone right back home, she has traveled through time. It is her son and her husband who are in the white car embedded under the bus. Adèle, whose name is not yet Adèle, is just about to undergo the ordeal of her final exams in information technology and management at the very moment when an accident befalls her husband and son on the old road leading to the lighthouse. Their car slipped down the cliff, soundlessly, it appears, since no one heard anything and for several days they were reported missing. Now Adèle has gone back to rescue them. Someone or something (maybe the snake) has given her this chance. She begins running toward the bus, which is strangely tilted, as if it were listening attentively to the asphalt. She throws herself at the rear door of the car, it does not open, she wrenches the handle, hears herself yelling, and finally uses her boots to break the window, and opens the door from inside. Her little boy has certainly grown, he must be fifteen now, he is unconscious, but he's alive all right, she can see the vein in his neck throbbing, his gaze is wild, his mouth open, his eyes dry.

Adèle's great body is like that of the snake that morning. It wriggles somehow or other to release the driver, it extracts the young man somehow or other and lays him down on the asphalt with a kiss on his brow (years later people who were on the bus will remember that kiss), it returns to the car but the adult is trapped, his legs and the dashboard have become fused together. The man looks at Adèle. He has big blue eyes, as blue as the sky that morning. He looks at her as one looks at one's child for the first time, as one looks at something infinitely beautiful and miraculous. He says, and his bleeding mouth gives him a voice full of bubbles, thank you, madame.

Blue eyes.

Thank you, madame.

Her husband had dark eyes. Her husband did not call her "madame." Adèle hears the fire department sirens and begins to weep. This is not at all what she had expected.

At the hospital two hours later the police are out in the corridor and Adèle, lying on her bed, knows they are there for her. They have given her a drip feed in her arm, she is waiting for the results of the X-ray of her back. Several people have come to congratulate her, to talk to her about what she remembers only vaguely. She recognizes skirts, mouths, handbags, pants. People stay with her for a while, some kiss her and say see you on Monday. One young man (big black earphones, white tracksuit, nylon backpack) sits beside her bed in silence for half an hour. A nurse gives her news: twenty-three people were more or less lightly injured, the children were well strapped in and the brakes on their strollers were firmly locked in place: Adèle was the only person to be flung out of the bus, several people are being kept in the hospital under observation, the driver of the car is in the operating room but "he is in stable condition," his son has recovered consciousness, he has nothing broken, he is hungry, he has asked to see Adèle. His mother and sister are with him. The nurse says it is a miracle.

Adèle repeats the word *miracle* several times in a soft voice until it no longer has any meaning. She feels helpless on this bed and can already picture what will happen to her, in five minutes, or an hour from now. Is this how it will all end? The police will come into her ward, they will question her, they will take her to the police station, and a day later, a week later, she will be deported. It will be simple, done smoothly, without bloodshed, and what can she say to avoid it? I'm sorry, I didn't come here to stay, I didn't come here to benefit from your handouts, I never intended to deceive you, I just wanted to disappear, that's all, I had no desire to deceive you, I had no desire to break the law, I thought it would be easier to die here. How can you explain the crazy actions of a woman who shaved her head, sold everything she possessed, paid for a two-week trip to Europe (Paris, Barcelona, Lisbon, London, Geneva), and stepped off the plane at Roissy airport one Saturday morning and never flew any further?

Deported. Up until now, in the subterranean world she inhabits, this word has been hovering above her without really touching her, as if it did not concern her, she who had burned her papers in the washroom in a hotel at Tours, or maybe it was Poitiers, she no longer recalls. A heap of gray ashes swirling around in the pan.

Up until now Adèle had done all she could not to exist, or, at least, to exist only minimally. The notion had never occurred to her that one day she would be plucked out from the hazy anonymity in which she existed and sent home (but where was it, this home, now?). She had learned to live like someone with no papers and, in truth, she realizes now, in this hospital bed, attached to this drip feed, it is thanks to this that she has survived. She has found a world parallel to that of those who are alive, who laugh, who make noise, normal people, people with identities. A soundless world where the inhabitants speak in whispers, walk by in silence, where doctors ask you neither your name nor your address, where dozens of intermediaries are there to arrange things (a place to stay, a job, a husband, a wife). A world with no contracts or signatures, no bank accounts, no vacations, no mail, a world where you are paid discreetly, a world with no plans, no dreams, no pity, no one to turn to, no friends, where everything is in cash, where everything has its price and where everybody can disappear from one day to the next. A world made for her.

Could it be that, by some kind of irony, she clings to this life? Could it be that the woman called Adèle actually exists a little?

Two policemen come in. They greet her and examine the notice attached to the foot of the bed. They note her false name.

"We've come to ask you a few questions, if you don't mind. Could you tell us what happened this morning?"

Adèle sits up and tells them simply and truthfully what she saw, what she remembers. One of the officers listens, with his hands behind his back, the other writes things down in a tiny notebook with a spiral binding, using a blue ballpoint pen. When she has finished she nods to them and turns away toward the window. She is waiting for them to ask for her real name, her address, her papers. She hears a movement in the room and the one who was listening with his hands behind his back goes out, the other one goes up to her. He has a lean face, without warmth but with no malice.

"You rescued a man and his son today."

"The father was trapped. I couldn't get him out."

"You stayed with him till the firefighters got there, you held his hand and talked to him. He's going to pull through."

"I don't remember."

"That's the shock. An accident always shakes you up."

He concludes by staring out of the window like her. At the end of the corridor there is a metallic noise, as if someone were bumping into a cart piled high with medical equipment, and the other police officer returns. The man with the lean face turns around.

"This is all in order. Madame lost her bag in the accident. She will come to the station tomorrow so we can take down her statement."

"Very good. Until tomorrow, madame, and congratulations on your bravery."

"Goodbye."

They leave unhurriedly, closing the door. The rays of the sun, broken up by the slats of the shutter, fall upon the ground, the bed, the bedside table, and Adèle's bag, plainly visible.

Later Adèle calls Cecilia Lesparet. It is 2:00 and Madame Lesparet is at home.

"I waited for you, Adèle. I telephoned. I left at least five messages! The children didn't want to go to school without you. I had to stay at home, I couldn't find anyone to take your place. They've been impossible all morning. I don't know what's got into them. I haven't had a minute to myself."

Cecilia Lesparet is pacing up and down in the kitchen. The children are watching a film in the living room, their minds and bodies immobilized for a moment. She knows it will only take a trifle for them to come to life again like hyperactive jumping jacks. She can hear her own rather grating voice quickly becoming

shrill (her own mother's voice). She knows she must be under-
standing, it was an accident, there *was* an accident, Adèle was
flung out of a bus, for heaven's sake, she is in the hospital, but
Cecilia cannot stop herself. She is still shaking from that cata-
clysmic morning when the clock had struck 8:00, and the children were so noisy, when the house was in chaos and she was
waiting, motionless, dressed, with her makeup on, in the kitchen.
She was fending off shouts from upstairs with an improvised
mantra: "Adèle's coming, Adèle's just coming, Adèle's going to be
here any minute now, Adèle will take care of it." But no. She didn't
come. She didn't call. She had dared not to.

Cecilia dreaded finding herself alone with her children, dreaded
things being like this every day, dreaded losing Adèle, this perfect nanny, who inspired the envy of all her friends. This was different from the constant and almost comforting fear of losing
her children or her husband, it is more like the dread of being
burgled while on vacation, or getting a scratch down the side of
her new car, or of the new coffee machine not matching up to the
price she paid for it.

When Cecilia had taken Adèle on seven years before (she
had answered the advertisement in impeccable, if somewhat
nineteenth-century, French), she had already tried out five nannies. She had only one child at the time. He was eighteen months
old and not yet walking. They lived in an apartment in the city
with a balcony that gave a partial view of the sea. Pascal had
installed three small cameras in the apartment without telling the nannies, the way they do in the United States, he said,
and at the end of each of their trial weeks the five nannies had
been thanked. Nothing serious: the child in front of the TV already in the morning, closets opened in the bedrooms, perfumes
sampled, the child left crying for a long time, the housework
hardly done, an afternoon nap taken in the master bedroom.

Then came Adèle in her Corsican widow's black dress, with her
soft voice and her shaven head. Cecilia remembers the pictures

from the cameras. She was certainly no Mary Poppins but, unlike the others, she took the child in her arms, she showed him things, and, above all, she played with him. Four days later the child had stood up on his two legs and toddled over to pick up a toy car.

They left the apartment, moved into the house, had two more children, changed jobs, went through a rocky patch in their marriage after the birth of the third, and made things up on a second honeymoon in the Maldives, but Adèle was always there somewhere, in the shadows on a photograph, in the corner of her eye, in the smell of the wax she polishes the furniture with on Fridays, in the perfect creases of the ironed sheets, in the way she manages the children's hair after it has been washed, the parting on one side, unfamiliar eau de cologne behind the ears. The children love that. Obliging Adèle, kind Adèle, discreet Adèle, perfect Adèle.

Adèle has never been late, has never failed to turn up, and did not even object when she learned about the cameras, and Cecilia pays her in cash. Oh, the recriminations their friends who did not film their nannies used to get involved in, forever ranting and complaining about them. The Lesparets never went on about the tedious routines of paperwork, claiming that their arrangement was one between consenting adults, like a free union. They could part company from one day to the next and because of this, *it is precisely because of this*, they used to say, this lack of any contract, of any formal constraints, that it worked. And their proof of this was seven years of good and faithful service and the three children in good health. Which one of their friends could show them such a track record?

They slipped her restaurant coupons, cinema tickets, some extra cash, double in December, gifts at Christmas, vacation souvenirs. Sometimes, when the holiday season was near, Cecilia would wonder whether she should get a little closer to Adèle, break the ice between employee and employer. *(So, tell me, Adèle: What are you doing for the holidays? Do you have a boyfriend, maybe a girlfriend, a cat?)* But she never did it, never found the right moment, and by the time it got to January 5 she was congratulating herself on this. She knew all she needed to know about Adèle: she looked after the children and the house well and was irreproachably honest.

"Five messages, Adèle. I left you five messages. So what time are you planning to come?"

Cecilia knows she should hold her peace but this is stronger than her. She feels betrayed. Instead of thinking about the number of times Adèle has helped them out at weekends, during vacations, at a moment's notice, instead of counting her days of absence (none), the times she has been late (fewer than five), Cecilia Lesparet is thinking about all those restaurant coupons slipped into the monthly envelope, the extra cash here and there, the designer clothes, the leather handbags, the chocolates, the macarons, the soaps, the perfumes, all the things she has been giving Adèle for years.

"Adèle? Are you there? I could come and pick you up if you like. Are you at the teaching hospital?"

On the far side of the city Adèle does not reply. Perched outside the window on a median strip there is a black crow. It gleams in the sunlight and looks enormous. For a moment nothing seems to be happening. Just this bird, motionless and shiny beneath the blue dome of the sky.

Do not Buddhists believe there are several moments contained within a single snap of the fingers and all it needs is an instant of awareness for you to wake up and change your life?

Adèle thinks about the moment when the door closed on the two policemen just now with a little click. Is such a moment all it takes? Does that little muted noise contain the whole of her future life?

The crow suddenly turns its powerful beak toward Adèle. It makes a swift, abrupt horizontal movement of its head. Once, twice, three times.

"No."

"Excuse me?"

"No. I can't come today. I need to rest."

"But you've no right to do that! Do you have a medical certificate?"

"Yes, I'll send it to you. I'm very sorry, Madame Lesparet, but I need to look after myself. I'll call you next week. Give the children a kiss from me."

Adèle hangs up, steps out into the soft light of this early March day. The crow is no longer there. Now everything is clear.

The concert

THE MOON HAS RISEN SOFTLY ABOVE THE HORIZON AND CASTS A pale yellow light over the sleeping city. The carousel is closed, the children are in bed, the chairs on the café terraces have been stacked away, the blinds on the stores lowered. A woman crosses the square rapidly, a shoulder bag held against her hip. She is wearing jeans, with a flowery silk top, a cotton jacket, and leather shoes so flat they look like dancing shoes. She has gathered her hair back into a ponytail. On the far side of the square, before walking down the few steps that lead to the Tropical's parking lot, she suddenly turns toward the sea and the moon lights up her face with a pale glow. Anita smiles.

When the singer with his dense mop of yellow hair begins shaking his *kayamb*, when the light picks him out with the dust whirling around him like sequins, when he begins his maloya chant, Anita and Adèle—one of them close to the stage, the other at the bar—both feel the same thrill pass through them. They do not understand all the words but these find a way deep into the pit of the stomach, precisely where for the first time each had felt her baby stirring—it is an inner effervescence. This creole blues awakens something within them that comes from far away, from the time when they used to dance free as air, when there were no lies, no dramas, when there were simply the endless, untroubled days of their childhood.

Anita hastily writes down in her notebook the lines that she wants to quote in her article. She is absorbing the totality of this concert: the palms raised to heaven, the heads bowed as if in prayer, the man close to her slowly swaying from right to left, his hands moving like waves, the straps of the dresses sliding over gleaming shoulders, the shirts clinging to backs, the smiles. The photographer from the paper is there as well, he greets her from afar, as if she were a colleague of long standing. She makes a note of the names of the instruments, the change of mood when the drum joins in, she exchanges a few words with some of the audience. She is often interrupted by the club's manager, Denis, who follows her everywhere, and seems interested above all, he says, in her "career path." He wants to know where she was born, when she came here, if she is married, how long she has worked on the paper.

At the end of the concert Anita meets the musicians back-stage, there is a holiday atmosphere, she is welcomed with open arms, they let her hold their instruments, they fall silent as she interviews the singer, who peers at her myopically through his thick glasses. The backup singers, superb young women, their fiery manes tied back with cotton scarves, smoke, argue, drink, or are simply there. These are women of the same age as Anita who eye her with benevolence. Anita would like to stay with them and ask them questions that have nothing to do with the concert: do they have husbands, children, how do they summon up the confidence and strength needed to leave their families for days at a time, how do they make sense of all those long hours on the road, the cramped backstage quarters, what is it that happens so mysteriously and magically when they are on stage? Anita feels like a friend, a sister of theirs, they are the same color.

When, regretfully, she takes her leave of the musicians, Denis offers her a drink. It is already 11:30. They are leaning against the bar and Denis beckons to the barmaid.

"What are you drinking?"

He accompanies his question with a gesture—tilting his head back with his thumb to his mouth.

"A Coke, please."

"A Coke? Come on! We have good homemade punch. We have beer from Mauritius, rum from Mauritius. It's on the house."

"It's very kind of you, monsieur, but I have to get back to the office to write my article. It appears tomorrow, you know."

Who does she think she is, this woman? Denis says to himself. For several days he has been broadcasting it to all and sundry, *the woman from the paper, the woman from the paper, the woman from the paper,* they had got on well on the telephone, he had made her laugh, something about rum and the heat, the classic quip he saves for customers who are native-born French, the well-worn cliché about islands, with their sleepy inhabitants and their easy life. It was the first time that an event organized at the club was going to be covered in the press and he was going to pamper her, this woman from the paper. He had evidently formed a very clear picture of her, this reporter, who called him "monsieur" on the telephone. Barely forty with half-length blond hair, one of those women who still wear ripped jeans and flaunt their bikinis on the beach. Possibly divorced, two teenage children, she watches American TV series with them, smokes a joint from time to time, never votes, but has an opinion on everything. Her face is beginning to show the signs of overexposure to the sun. She likes dancing, prefers the company of men to that of women, she's white. When Anita appeared before him and introduced herself he felt almost vexed, as if he had been cheated on the goods he had ordered.

So, how had she got here? Was she born here? What schooling had she had? How old was she? He would never have ventured questions like this with anyone else but, as he himself had a grandmother from Mauritius, he has the curiosity of a distant relative. But Anita sidesteps, she responds to his questions with other questions, and suddenly he gets the message. She's assimilated.

Oh yes, he's met others like her, these immigrants who've gone far beyond what was expected of them, who live either in the center of the city or in some village in the forest, they have houses in the country, they go to Paris for the holidays, they don't have a trace of an accent. They smear themselves with sunscreen all summer because they don't want to tan even if no one can see the difference, they know the fashionable restaurants, marry locals, call their children Clovis or Marianne, are experts at tasting wine, love runny cheese, and can't abide chili peppers anymore. They never come to the Tropical, they go to the Cercle, downtown, which plays sanitized and packaged world music on Friday nights. When these assimilated immigrants meet a compatriot they smile faintly, as people do at the poor, the ignorant, the unfortunate. The woman from the paper had done just that when he asked her *precisely* where on Mauritius she had been born.

A Coke! Whatever next? (A milkshake?)

"So I guess you're like the cops in the movies, are you? You don't drink when you're on duty?"

And suddenly she laughs. All at once she reminds him of those shy young women who hide their mouths when they laugh, as if they had bad teeth. Maybe he'd judged her too hastily? It's clear she's eager to write a good article.

"All right. Just a tiny glass of punch."

Denis leans across the bar and literally yells: "Adèle! Adèle!"

Then he turns back to Anita and she smiles at him in the most open and dazzling manner possible.

"The barmaid comes from Mauritius, like you."

"Is that so? I really like your club. I'll come back here."

Denis had definitely been mistaken that evening.

Anita delivers her copy at 1:00 in the morning. Fifteen minutes later the news editor calls her to tell her in a warm voice that all is well, the piece is "perfect," and she can go home.

But Anita lingers in the empty reporters' room. She walks over to the big bay windows that look out over the square, she strolls around, inhaling deeply, as if she wanted to breathe it all in and keep it within herself: the Post-it notes stuck to screens, the titles of books on desks, the personal photographs pinned up with thumbtacks or in frames, the quotations on the walls, the posters, the tourist pictures. She keeps her hands behind her back, as in a museum, so as to touch nothing, disturb nothing. Anita likes this place and can still feel the effects of the adrenalin, that mixture of excitement and stage fright when she had to sit down and write, when she had to condense everything she had seen, learned, and felt during the evening into five hundred words. But when her fingers began tapping away, everything around her had disappeared. Oh, the feeling of being a woman engaged in creation, one who is unsinkable, useful, one who does her work well, and is fully present in every one of her thoughts, her emotions, her desires!

When she leaves the building she is still clinging a little to this euphoria, as one clings to the lingering haze of sleep, she does not want to go back home right away, she wants to go on being this blossoming, independent woman for a little longer. She knows that in a few hours' time, things will become real, less romantic. With a firm but light tread she retraces her footsteps. Anita goes back into the club. She wants to listen to music, sip an elegant amber alcoholic drink (alone at 1:00 in the morning! after writing her first story as a real reporter!).

Inside there are fewer people than earlier on and the music now is disco. The musicians of the group from Réunion have left. They had another concert to go to the next day thirty miles away. Anita is aware of a sudden impulse to run after them, follow them, linger in the warm, golden wake of their music. Would she have given in to this impulse if she had been younger, with no husband, no child? Anita likes to think that at the age of thirty-five she would still have had the courage to do it, as she likes to believe that, as of tomorrow, she could abandon all her bourgeois comforts, live in a tent, start all over again.

She settles on a stool, one elbow on the bar. All the vibrant animal energy—those figures standing there with uplifted arms, that music—has vanished and it is as if she were in a totally different place now, and had dreamed it all. Nothing catches her eye, no colors, no shapes, though Anita is not impervious to such things. She is floating in some kind of aura that is soft, hazy, maybe a little sad, an aura with a stale smell of alcohol. Good and evil, light and darkness, success and failure, responsibilities and freedom, doubt and conviction, family and solitude, fervor and cowardice, equality and submissiveness, none of this exists anymore.

Suddenly.

An arm, a gleam of light on a silver bracelet, the tall figure of a woman dressed in black, a face dominated by a moving mouth. Open, shut, open.

"I'm sorry? I didn't hear."

"I was asking if you'd like something to drink. I'm going to close the bar soon. I still have some punch left."

"Yes, it was very good, that punch. What's your name, by the way?"

This question came out as softly as a breath of air, something emerging from who knows where and settling between two people.

"Adèle."

"Adèle . . . that's pretty."

"It's not my real name, you know."

That, too, came out as calmly as hello, how are you today, what would you like. Adèle feels a tingling all over her body, but she does not fall to the ground, she does not flinch, nor is this, as they say in books, a moment of truth.

"No?"

"No."

"Look. I won't drink anything. But may I stay here for a moment?"

"Sure. We close in half an hour."

"Are you going home after that?"

"Yes."

"Would you like to have a stroll on the beach with me? It's not cold at all. After that, I'll drop you off. I have a car."

"Okay."

"So what's your real name?"

"I'll tell you another time."

And the element of chance in all this, the ease that is established between two women who have only just met, is no small thing. Anita looks back at the room with new eyes. Now she notices the shadowy figures on the sofas, a woman dancing out in the full light, a man in the half light at the edge of the dance floor waiting for some sign, a tune, another tempo, before he goes to join her. No, it is not true that there is nothing here. Here, too, there are years, hours, and the same sentimental crowd clinging to its dreams.

Adèle and Anita sit there, the two of them, looking out to sea. The night is cool, there is this perfectly round moon, tinged with gray, with beige, with pink, there is the sound of the waves. In this moment, which is both simple and extraordinary, Adèle glimpses another way of living, another way of loving, giving, weeping, laughing, working, starting again.

Adèle decides she will not tell lies to Anita as she lies to other people. She will tell her her real name, she will tell her her life story, talk about her husband and her son. On the beach, in the utter purity and nakedness of this moment, something is released deep within her, a knot slowly unraveling itself and she breathes deeply. The night fills her.

Yet between them that night there are no revelations, no secrets shared, no solemn vows. They speak the way the waves are breaking down below, without hesitation, but with no haste either.

Long silences occur that do not trouble them. Adèle tells her what she does: three nights at the Tropical, days at the Lesparets.

A hardworking and lonely life emerges in the short, simple sentences she uses.

"Do you get on well with the children?"

"Yes. But I don't know if I'll continue with it. I was in an accident this morning."

"What happened?"

"A bus I was on crashed into a car. I was thrown out."

"What? My goodness! But are you all right? You still came to work?"

"Some people were injured, but I was fine. I was just a bit bruised on my back."

"But that's a miracle! To be unscathed after being thrown out from a bus!"

A miracle. How many times has she heard that word today? How many times between this Saturday now and that Tuesday so long ago has she prayed for one? A miracle.

"What does 'unscathed' mean?"

"Hmm . . . It means without any injuries. But it also means that you're a survivor."

A "survivor." Adèle rolls the word around in her mouth and for her this has the same effect as a creole word tasted after so many years, something both sweet and strong at the same time.

A boat passes by out there upon the dark sea. With winking lights it moves toward the line of the horizon. Maybe people on this boat are gazing at the land, leaning on the rail, their eyes fixed on the lights that trace the contours of the city. Where are they bound for, what are they thinking about, what are they saying, what are they hiding? Can they sense the presence of two women sitting on the beach, their silhouettes like two motionless rocks?

"Do you miss our country, Adèle?"

"No. Do you?"

"Yes, sometimes. But I can never figure out exactly what it is I miss. It's strange. It's like thinking about people you knew long ago. You can no longer picture their faces but you remember things they did, things they said. The odd phrase, the odd gesture."

Then Adèle thinks about her son. She no longer remembers his face but she can still smell his warm, sweet breath in the morning, when he was a baby, she can picture his favorite toy, a bright red wooden car, she can hear him babbling, she pictures the white Fiat driving away and her son's arm waving goodbye to her. But she can no longer picture his face.

In the car Anita offers Adèle a throw for her legs. On the backseat there are coloring books, a child's seat, rubber boots. Anita apologizes. "It's an old car," she says. "Don't look at all that mess," she says again. Then, before starting the engine, she asks: "Would you mind if we drove around a little before I drop you off?"

Adèle is surprised and appreciative of being spoken to like this, close at hand, as if she were a normal woman, a person who might be offended by disorder, or have cold legs, an ordinary woman with an ordinary life who might be in a hurry to get home.

Anita's car slips slowly through the night, drives along streets lined with ancient trees, passes through the center of the city, drives around the big park where during the day one can sometimes see the long necks of giraffes among the trees. The night air, so deep and soothing, fills the car. There is nothing to be said, except, perhaps, thank you.

The car passes back along the avenue that runs beside the sea, then finally heads off toward the bypass, the industrial zones, land left fallow, wasteland. She stops just beside the bus stop where Adèle had been standing that morning. Where is that snake now? Can one's life change in a day? Does a single day like that suffice for one to say "enough" and for one to end up, at last, by turning the page?

The world as Laura sees it

LAURA IS SIX. HER FATHER MAKES WOODEN HORSES FOR HER, WHICH they paint together in all colors, also a dream catcher made of little pinecones and feathers that hovers gently in the window, and a white desk, a cradle for her dolls, a fruit and vegetable seller's market stall, a little cabin in the garden. When he takes her out for a walk in the forest she carries a little basket for pinecones, twigs, leaves. She likes gathering pinecones with a perfect V. Sometimes, if they find a dead bird, they make a bed of supple branches for it and cover it with ferns. Laura likes it when her father lets her stay in his studio for a little while, as he is putting things away or reading. He clears one end of the table, gives her sheets of paper and pencils, and she would like this moment (inextricably associated with the smell of turpentine and the color yellow) to last forever, and *forever* is a word she loves a lot. He tells her to be careful of the paint, because it leaves a mark, and of the brushes, which are heavy to hold, and he teaches her the different shades of color. Carmine, chocolate, magenta, mustard, purple. He always studies her drawings closely before smiling at her and asking her precise questions to which, inexplicably, she finds the answer. He does not hang up her drawings, unlike her mother, but stores them in an orange folder, and, later on, a green folder. In the car he sometimes takes her on his knee and lets her hold the wheel. He tells her tales of things that happened right here, in this forest, under this very sky, to this wooden toy.

When he carries her on his shoulders he holds onto her calves and she can wrap her hands around his face. Laura likes to view the world from up there, with people looking up and smiling at her, and she is proud, strong, and light.

Laura is six. Her mother wakes her up every morning by saying, *bonjour, ma petite chérie*, and blowing on her fingers, along her arms, her neck, behind her ear; she reads her stories every evening, she sings and dances, she makes marvelous afternoon snacks with chocolate cookies, syrups, peeled and cut up fruits, and sandwiches of white, sliced bread cut into geometric shapes, with white napkins, all carefully stored away in airtight boxes, as if they were treasure. Her mother tells her stories involving sand, the sea, trees that are good for climbing and hiding in, stories in which the sun is so hot it can cook an egg and make the roadway melt. She says one day we'll go there. She says I must teach you the creole language. She cleans Laura's toes with a little brush shaped like a crocodile, she tells her the names of plants, she stops the car for them to pick bunches of wildflowers, or just to look at a meadow. She is very patient about getting her to eat, cutting things into little pieces, inventing songs and little tricks. She lets Laura draw in her study while she is working and Laura knows how to be quiet, hoping that this moment will last forever. Her mother still carries her on one hip, supporting her bottom with her forearm. Laura likes her mother's strength for she can carry her like this for a long time and still do other things with her other hand. Laura remains silent when she is carried like this, so close to her mother's body that she can smell her sweet scent. She can feel the slightest quivering of the muscles, the hollow of the hip she is perched on, and she has the same light, joyful sensation as on her father's shoulders.

Laura is too young to be aware of the magical nature of her house, of her bedroom that is like no other—there is a hatch inside her wardrobe that leads to another hatch inside her parents' wardrobe and sometimes, when she has friends to tea, her mother allows them to play at passing through from one room into another—her wooden toys, her birds on the wall, her little princess's cabin in the garden. She likes going to see her best friend, Sophie, whose parents have an apartment in the city with a big TV and wall-to-wall carpet in the living room. She could spend hours at the window watching the cars speeding along on the boulevard down below.

Her mother talks to her, with many an "oh" and "ah" and "hmm," about the faraway island where she was born, but Laura has never been there on the plane, she only knows the car in which they sometimes drive for hours on end—her parents call it going for a spin. All the time they keep saying look, Laura, look— they go to the sea, to the mountains, to the lake. In the winter they light a fire in the fireplace and perform puppet plays written by her mother.

"Where is my prince?"

"He's been swallowed by the dragon! It's all over for him. Kaput."

"What am I going to be when I grow up?"

"You'll be president of the republic!"

Sometimes she would prefer things to be simpler, for the princess to be reunited with her prince and for the dragon to be killed with the sword of truth and love.

Laura is a little girl people call "good." She is not one of the ones people swoon over. She has a frank stare that can be unsettling, as if she knew things, as if she has a sixth sense about the nature of men and women. Her parents would like to glimpse what she carries within herself: her mother's passion, her father's good looks, a talent for perceiving and transforming, an original mind, a luminous spirit? They are impatient to see her grow up, impatient to know what elements of themselves she will carry within her.

It is in the evenings above all that Laura wishes she could be with them. When the hour for her bedtime has long since struck, when the books have been read, the kisses given, the day talked through, the songs sung, and she can hear her parents living another life down below. There they are talking, laughing, sometimes arguing, drinking and eating, watching films and listening to music, and on some evenings when sleep will not come, she feels as if she were a total stranger to them, as if she could disappear, no longer exist, and they would not notice her absence. Later on her mother comes softly upstairs and closes the door to her study. Her father goes out and she sees his tall figure walking, softly as well, across the grass, and a moment later the lights come on in his studio. What they do at night, each of them in their own space, is something mysterious from which she is kept firmly at a distance.

Her mother has less time these days. She talks on the phone a lot—with a much more animated and high-pitched voice than usual—she is never far from her diary and on occasion she argues with her father about this. She has a meeting and so has he, *what is to be done about the child?*

The child the child the child.

She wishes they would stop calling her that. She would like a dog, a little sister, she believes the secret promises she makes there in her bed at night (if I have a sister, I'll stop listening at doors; if I have a dog, I'll stop looking through your stuff, *Maman*). At school they ask her why her mother is black and when she goes home and puts this question to Anita she replies crisply: "I'm not black, I'm brown. Can't you tell the difference?"

She feels both poor and rich, both adored and neglected. She has all she could wish for and is alone.

Then at the start of spring she meets Adèle.

It is a Saturday afternoon and fine enough for her to play in the garden. A checkered tablecloth, a frilly dress, shoes with heels, bracelets, a tiara. Real little cookies on little blue plates, real fruit juice in the red teapot. Her father is sitting cross-legged and she has just made him put on a cardboard crown that she had saved from their Twelfth Night celebrations.

"Would you like another cookie, Your Majesty?"

"With great pleasure, Your Highness. This is delicious. Did you make them yourself?"

"Yes, Your Majesty. I used flour, eggs, sugar, and chocolate chips baked in the oven. Would you like some fruit juice?"

"Yes please, Your Highness."

Adam and Laura are more than transformed. They are magically transfigured by the game, the dressing up, the setting, the green lawn scattered with dozens of cloverleafs, all the tiny things that have to be held with the tips of the fingers, this cup, this saucer, this perfect moment. The truth is, thinks Adam, it is our children who raise us onto a higher plane, there will never be any painting, any monument, any house, any friendship, any lover, any book that can match this. Laura hears the clatter of Anita's car pulling up and is disappointed. She knows her mother's arrival will interrupt the game. Anita will be tired. She will want a cup of tea, her father will, as well, and they will end up saying what they always say to her, *go and play on your own for a little while.*

"Hi there! Cooee!"

Anita is not alone. A big, tall woman is following her. As the two of them come walking through the wisteria arbor with the light behind them it looks as if Anita has a giant shadow.

Adam and Laura remain rooted to the spot for a moment at the sight of this curious phenomenon. Then the woman steps aside, Laura moves closer to her father, who gets to his feet and picks her up in his arms. They still have the crown and the tiara on their heads.

"Adèle, this is my husband, Adam. And the little princess here is Laura. Adam, this is Adèle, the lady I told you about."

Adam reflects that she has a face like those of the goddesses in the Cour de Richelieu at the Louvre. He has an impulse to run his hands over the perfectly formed, downy crown of her head. What has gotten into him?

"Come along. Let's have a cup of tea indoors. Laura, could you go and play on your own for a little while?"

Adam sets Laura down on the lawn. A cup has spilled on the tablecloth. Everything is spoiled.

Suddenly this amazingly gentle voice emanates from Adèle's massive frame.

"Why don't we take tea out here with the princess?"

Three adults and a child have a dolls' tea party. She is like a *tableau vivant*, thinks Adam. Her story is incredible, thinks Anita. I'm a real princess, thinks Laura. This is a dream, thinks Adèle.

A dinner

THEY WILL BE HAVING DINNER IN THE GARDEN. THIS, ANITA SAYS TO herself, as she admires the table, fully laid, is just the kind of thing that she should be handing on to Laura as her heritage. The patchwork of a whole life. The silver service from her parents-in-law, the royal blue plates she had picked up in an antique shop in Paris, the Basque tablecloth bought in a mountain village when covering a story, the white table napkins embroidered with her parents' initials (S and P) entwined, glasses that were a wedding present, the table made by André, Adam's father, the chairs retrieved from a yard sale and fixed up by Adam, a bouquet gathered in the meadow by Adèle in a cheap vase picked up at the supermarket, coasters made from bamboo.

Here and there in the garden Adam had set up poles with solar lights. As night fell they would be glowing softly like stars fallen from the sky.

She would like to capture under a dome this moment when everything is in suspense, perfect, like a flower bud about to open and reveal its promise to the world. It is the start of summer and this year, the year when she will be thirty-seven, Anita is the beating heart of her home and her family. She washes and polishes, she changes the curtains, she does the cooking, she starts wearing her bracelets again, she gets out her long gypsy skirts. She takes her siestas out of doors, where the grass is as thick as a carpet, she makes Adèle laugh, she is healing her with her friendship, her time, her house. She often clings to Adam, gives him passionate kisses, she is rediscovering the thrilling sensations of long ago, ones that bore into the base of the spine and make her toes spread out like a fan. She finds him handsome, she admires him, she has an amazing sense of being more in love with him than ever, she is happy. Anita feels she has found her way, is on the right road, she welcomes this exciting new life, one in which she works, writes, loves, has extra energy. Since Adèle came everything has changed. She looks after Laura when Anita and Adam are working; she cooks, she sews, she encourages, she mends, she loves them. She bathes their house in a serenity that was hitherto lacking, she gives the family that little bit extra that oils the wheels of daily life, lightens routine, and makes the windows gleam. But that is not all.

Since Adèle came, Anita is writing. She has returned to her notebooks, she has been doing research, listening, taking notes, and, one evening in spring, started work on, *shh*, a novel. Chapter one, chapter two, the impulse does not fade, Anita is finally in possession of that mysterious thing—something beyond strength, courage, inspiration, tenacity, something that does not interfere with household tasks, motherhood, parenting, love, the body, sexual desire, dreams, hopes—the thing that makes her set down one word after another, one sentence and then another, one page and then another, without losing heart, without self-denigration. Adèle has set Anita free to write. But this is not all.

Since Anita came, Adam has begun another series of paintings, inspired by Adèle's story and the first pages of Anita's text. He has cast aside brushes, spray cans, pencils, palettes. He has only made two paintings so far. He is no longer striving to imitate a landscape or a face, but to evoke an emotion, a texture, a taste. He works more slowly than usual, but this new path is enthralling.

On this first Saturday of the summer vacation Adam and Anita are entertaining their friends, a ritual that goes back quite a few years now. People they met in Paris, in the humanities department, at the school of architecture, in an editorial office, in a café, these are people now approaching their forties, still with young children and elderly parents, and secret lives, that's for sure. From one year to the next they notch up little changes (a few pounds overweight, a child born, a love affair falling apart, the death of a parent), but when they arrive at Anita and Adam's house, when their cars start bouncing over the first pinecones, when the house itself comes into view, gleaming like a flagship at the end of the avenue, when they see Anita, Adam, and Laura on the doorstep, they feel both happy and envious.

They know what will fascinate them yet again: Adam's triptych in the living room, painted at the time of Laura's birth. Within a great frame of dark wood there are sketches of three scenes. The first in pearly gray, the second in midnight blue, the third in emerald green. The first shows a soldier in helmet and boots sitting in a trench, his gas mask around his neck, his head bowed over a letter held on his knee; the second shows a man running, seen from behind, his head turned to look over his shoulder, as if he were checking to see if he is being followed, his long coat flung open as he moves; the third sketch is of a man in ripe old age, smiling, his two hands lightly resting on a walking stick. Above him, giving him its shade, there is a spreading tree. Behind him, a forest.

Each picture is deceptively simple and nobody knows how this is contrived, whether it is the clear, bold lines or the color, but they seem alive and vibrant. At each dinner, every summer, new details come to light. In the first sketch there is a faint touch of pink about the letter, and, when this is finally noticed, it is not just a color, but also a perfume, a flower, a love letter, a promise. In the second sketch the man has bare feet and that, too, is not noticeable at first glance. There is movement in the drawing, the coat opening out like a pair of wings, the face both resolute and uneasy, looking straight at you and suddenly, this vulnerability of the bare feet. Beside the third man there is a wooden cube, a child's toy, and if you get closer to it you can make out the image of a dark-brown pinecone.

The friends already know what will make them jealous: the house. Not that it is particularly beautiful, but it has a heart, it is young as well as being old and wise, a little rickety, furnished haphazardly, a treasure here, a piece of junk there. The passing years have seen it settling into its site, it both imposes and pampers.

The friends know exactly what they will encounter this evening: books, pictures, sketches, timber, both cool and warm, fine worn carpets, beautiful photographs in painted wooden frames, a child's drawings, cushions decorated with little mirrors, flowers everywhere, dozens of jam jars filled with little dark stones, seashells, sand, and translucent pebbles in pastel shades picked up on the beach, perfumed candles, music, a fine table, fine glasses in which they will swirl a good wine beneath a multitude of soft lights, a good meal.

Oh, all this could be irritating at times. All these books, these pictures, the garden, the couple themselves, the wine "from a little vineyard not far from here," the *parmigiana di melanzane* with eggplants from the garden, the basmati rice, the mangoes, sweet as honey, bought heaven knows where, a "typical" dessert from Mauritius, a touch of theater about the whole thing. But there is never any vanity about these evenings, Anita and Adam are warmly welcoming, they are happy to see them, they make great efforts for everything to please them, they ask countless questions about Paris, about the other cities, about what is going on out there, about an exhibition, a play, a film, about what they are all doing in their lives, in their daily lives. Maybe Anita will surprise them by asking:

"Describe one of your days to me."

"Oh, you know, it's not very interesting."

"No, no. Tell me in detail. What time do you get up? What do you have for breakfast? . . ."

And because Anita asks this without irony, with real interest, they will tell it. The toast, the salted butter, the coffee knocked back, the child who is currently in floods of tears every morning, the relief when it can be left at the nursery school, the line they take on the metro, the names of colleagues, a piece of juicy gossip . . . They are amazed at everything they find themselves telling, or, at least, to be recalling details they were not aware of noticing at the time.

Naturally the children will end up bringing out a few mattresses into the garden, beneath canvas sheets slung between the trees, naturally they will be wide-eyed with glee at staying up late and playing outside, naturally they will do some dancing. Naturally their friends will talk about themselves as they once were, about what they are now, their present lives, naturally they will use the phrase "in the old days" and will toy with the notion of doing what Anita and Adam have done, moving to the country. On the word *country*, they will wax eloquent, making sweeping gestures to embrace the house, the garden, the arbor, the forest, Anita, Adam. Naturally they will say all that, but later on . . .

Without making any comment they will be noticing Adam's hands, stained like a painter's, rough and broad like a workman's. The women will dwell for a moment on Anita's clothes and shoes—out-of-date colors, unfashionable styles, jackets made of rough wool, worn-down heels, all things bought at markets, like their cheese, their joss sticks, their Afghan *pakol* caps. They will reflect on the two cars parked in the lane, country vehicles, dirty, noisy, battered. They will end up admiring, but not envying, liking but not being tempted.

Finally the moment will come, well past midnight, when they feel the need to get up and go. They will pick up their children in their arms and lay them down head to tail on the backseat, no thanks, they won't stay, their hotel or their rented house is not far away, they will exchange kisses amid loud laughter, in the end someone will sound his horn. Of course they will be a little sad, but as they leave behind the lane strewn with pinecones, with their headlights picking out the trunks of the trees and the ferns, all of this (the countryside, the deep silence, the forest, everything handmade) will suddenly seem intolerable. It will strike them that Anita and Adam are living lives in the past, outmoded, that make no sense, and then they will begin to drive a little too fast, back toward their beds, their rented rooms, and start thinking about their apartments in the city, the noise of the metal shutters on the stores, the supermarket shelves, the famous actress glimpsed on the metro, and that possibility of being alone amid a noisy crowd.

This year there are some ten adults, with just the same quantity of children, shouts of greeting, hugs, and exclamations of delight as in previous years. Like well-brought-up guests and good friends, they comment on small changes: Anita has a new hairstyle and has gone back into pretty outfits, Adam has grown a fine beard, the kitchen garden has been enlarged, the child's cabin in the garden has been repainted. On the way, before they got there they saw bulldozers, what's going on? It's a housing development, says Adam, and they all adopt a horrified air, what a scandal that people should want to live here!

Adam enjoys these evenings less and less. Having now lost his father, despite his sadness, he has a greater sense of freedom. He is no longer the little boy whose shyness must be excused, he is no longer the clumsy youth whom people coerce into playing rugby or tennis, he is no longer the boy who likes painting. That morning he had asked Anita: "Do you enjoy seeing them again?"

"Yes, of course. What about you?"

"I don't know. Do you think they're friends, real friends?!"

Anita had thought about Julie, Barbara, Nicolas. Those evenings so long ago, sitting on the floor, the arguments at corner cafés, the love affairs, the tears, and all that energy expended, wasted, for what, if the truth be told? Just because they were young, because they thought they were irresistible?

"We've all changed, Adam."

"Okay. But it gets on my nerves."

When they arrive and the women gather in the kitchen, the men in the garden, Anita feels she should make some effort to retrieve the thread of this friendship, and draw it right out into the open, at the center of things, and she talks nonstop. She keeps asking questions and suddenly she realizes that, for their part, Julie, Barbara, Anne, and the others are replying offhandedly, as if Anita were being indiscreet. She leans over the sink to wash the salad (young shoots of beetroot, spinach, and watercress) and falls silent. An unpleasant feeling of déjà vu overcomes her, she knows exactly how the evening is going to go, who will talk more than the others, what topics will provoke heated debates. She will not mention her novel, Adam will say nothing about his painting. Not to them. What was it Adam had asked that morning? Are they real friends?

Then Anita sees Adèle at the bottom of the garden and it warms her heart. She thinks about the time they spent by the lake the previous day, a magical day, warm and bright. During the summer, when there is throbbing heat from the morning onward, when the cars form lines of gleaming metal all along the road that leads to the beach, when the smell of fritters, sandwiches, and crepes overlays those of salt and wind, Anita, Adam, and Laura go to the lake, barely two miles from their house. They could go on foot but in the summer they take their bicycles and a picnic and thread their way along sandy lanes and footpaths strewn with pine needles, past the delicate, lacy fronds of ferns. Again yesterday the lake was waiting for them, so bright and still. The gray jetty, the flat stones, already a little cracked by the heat. There, stretched out on the stones, as if they were the only women in the world, they had talked without fear. Adèle had continued telling her story, the story that so sets Anita's heart beating. The little girl was playing in the shadow of the pine trees, Adam was swimming across the lake, and the noise of his strokes reached them, marking a rhythm to their conversation. That same evening, replete with Adèle's words, Anita had reopened her notebook. She had the feeling of an urgent need to absorb this story and tell it in a new form.

Suddenly Barbara asks her a question.

"So how about you, Anita? What are you up to? Are you still writing articles about Basque pelota matches?"

For his part, Adam cannot help silently studying the men in his garden, with their fine shoes, their excessively tight jeans, their mauve or pink shirts, their mouthfuls of clichés about the grass, the fruits, the harsh winters here, the mentality of the local people, and then their questions about work, while Adam has no desire to talk about work, about plans, projects, inviting bids. Then he, too, catches sight of Adèle and thinks about their time beside the lake on the previous day. After their return he had shut himself away in his studio to begin the third painting in his new series. This woman fascinates him. In her presence his fingers tingle, his vision blurs, he rediscovers the impulse to paint as in the old days, before technique, before knowledge, before fashion. A while ago now he had laid a bare stretched canvas on the floor in the middle of his studio. He had poured black paint onto it until this formed an irregular circle on the picture. Then he spent a long time looking at this black circle that shone like a mirror and thinking about Adèle. The following day he had meticulously chosen a red, had mixed it with a little white, a little black, a hint of pink. Then he went into a corner and began pouring the paint as if he wanted to make a line of color across the canvas passing over the frame. Except that he slowed down, speeded up, backtracked, stopped for a few seconds, his eyes shut, his eyes open. He had called this first painting *Melody*.

Drinks are served as they stand in the garden. Adam's studio, which attracts curiosity (and teasing toward the end of the evening, what have you got hidden there? Come on, show us!) is still firmly closed, the curtains drawn. There is the beautiful lawn, the wooden chairs, the awnings stretched taut, the candles on the tables, the children in the playhouse, air that is both dense and fresh, something one can feel going deep into one's lungs and acting there like an air freshener, they exchange news, they drink a toast, they stroll around a little, they light the first cigarettes. There is, after all, something gratifying about this start to the evening. A year has passed and they are all still there, no one has been forgotten, there has been no great disaster, no revolution, no great quarrels, no, they are still the same, or almost, at the start of this evening with all the children running in and out between their legs. They have the feeling that there is a special glamour about ordinary life, routine, traditions (getting married, having children, going on vacation, seeing friends, being in good health, little girls wearing smocked dresses and little boys wearing Bermuda shorts), and they feel grateful.

Julie is the first to notice Adèle. Going up to Anita, and in the brisk tone of voice she sometimes adopts, she remarks: "Anita, there's a woman in your kitchen."

Anita looks up and sees Adèle in the doorway.

They all turn to watch her approaching. Adèle walks slowly because Laura and the other children are dancing around her, as if she had promised them candies. They all notice her towering figure, her muscular, bare arms, effortlessly carrying a crate filled with bottles, her long solid legs in tight-fitting black jeans, her black boots. The gold of the setting sun pours down from the sky, filters through the leaves of the lilac trees, and spills onto Adèle's shaven head. There is the bracelet that sinks into her flesh a little when she sets the crate down on the ground. There is her Madonna-like face, her discreet and simple smile, her eyes slightly lowered, the hand she presses to her heart when she straightens up, and then Laura throws herself into her arms. Now she smiles broadly at Anita and at Anita alone. There is something other than friendship between these two women, there is a country, pictures beyond words, gestures beyond dissection, the little memories of childhood, the little memories of a country left behind, when the bread was like that and bus tickets were this color, when that was what we used to say, when this was what we used to do, when these were the fruits we used to eat.

Adèle turns on her heel and walks away, with the brood of children in tow, without a word, without a glance at the others.

"My God! What style! Who is that girl?"

Anita feels shaky, as if she has stepped onto a fracture in a rock. On the one hand there is her daughter running off, happy and laughing with Adèle (was Laura ever as merry in her company?); on the other hand there are her husband and their friends who seem to be hypnotized by Adèle. For once in her life she would have liked to experience having that effect on people, men, women, and children all alike. Does it make you strong? Invincible? Vain? Happy? Brave?

She tries to think back to the days of her youth, when she had just arrived in Paris, when she spent hours walking along the quays, sat on the green benches in the parks and wrote, offered her face to the sun, stretched out on the grass, when she spent hours talking on café terraces, coffee, cigarettes, and ideas. Was she beautiful at the time? She turns and catches Adam's eye. Something infinitely tender and mysterious passes between them. All their various lives seem to be in harmony at last, the newspaper and the novel; the architecture and the painting; being parents and being selfish; being full of vitality and on the brink of forty.

"Who'd like some punch? It's a home brew."

"Punch? That's a bit 1980s, isn't it?"

That New Year's Eve party in a house in Montreuil, a green sofa, punch that was far too strong. Anita and Adam smile.

"So who's that chick? Is she Laura's nanny or is she a relative of yours, Anita? I hope she's going to join us later."

It is Alexandre who puts the question. He is wearing electric-blue velvet shoes with a straw hat on his head. He is a lawyer.

Adam sighs and images of a younger Alexandre appear before his eyes. An Alexandre hopelessly in love with some girl, but who, even in the midst of the exquisite agonies of a passion not wholly reciprocated, cut a droll figure. In those days his fickle heart used to amuse them, the way he would seduce, abandon, weep, deceive, return.

Adam opens his mouth but it is Anita who replies.

"So, because she's not white she must either be the nanny or a relative of mine? On a point of clarification, my learned friend, don't you think that remark is based on a somewhat racist presumption?"

There is an instant of stupefied silence (Anita? Was it Anita who said that?) until Adam gives a great guffaw and the others burst out laughing as well. But that moment was enough for everyone to grasp that things have changed in that house on the edge of the forest and it is not just a change of hairstyle, or a beard being allowed to grow, or a garden being enlarged.

Today

ANITA HAS PLACED THE FILE ON THE KITCHEN TABLE AND EYES IT as if it were a dangerous animal temporarily asleep. She has only a little time, Laura has dozed off but that won't last. All those years in the attic have not altered either the blue of the file or the strength of the cotton strap that holds it together. Nor have they erased the title, written across it by her hand in black felt pen.

The Melody of Adèle.

She had, as she promised Adam, erased the text from her computer, but she had kept a printout of it in a cardboard box in the attic. What is to be done with this now? Throw it in the fire? Tear up every page one by one until her fingers bleed, turn it into confetti to blow away across the forest?

Things would have been so different if only she had listened to Adam. Right at the start, when she had written just a few pages, he had advised her to talk about it to Adèle. In Adam's mouth the words had a disarming simplicity, *Adèle, I should like to write your story.* But Anita had never found the right moment and the words remained stuck in her throat like a lump of hard bread. The months went by, she wrote, she asked questions, she listened, she made notes, she checked and wrote some more. Then Adam started painting and the two of them turned into thieves, imposters, traitors, liars.

Anita would so like to hate this ill-omened object, to be able to spit on it, hurl it against the wall, but oh, the absolute tenderness she brings to merely touching the thing is heartrending. She runs her hand gently over the blue of the file, she undoes the strap. Just a page, she tells herself, just one. After that, promise, she will throw it away.

A breath of magic is released and she cannot stop herself. What is it? A perfume, the memory of what it had been to write those words? Has the ghost of the old Anita just settled on her shoulder, or is it Adèle's spirit?

Title: The Melody of Adèle

CHAPTER 1

When I was little and they asked me what I wanted to do when I grew up, I used to say I'd like to work in an office. My friends always said things like astronaut, airline pilot, TV presenter, prime minister, sailor on a submarine. It seems to me that even when I was little I didn't want anything extraordinary or unbelievable to happen to me. You see when I thought of things being "extraordinary" or "unbelievable" I'd think of my uncle who enlisted in the First World War and came back with half his face missing. When my parents and all the family talked about him they always used to say, "What he did was unbelievable!" "What a hero! What an extraordinary life!" When I knew him, he was already a very elderly gentleman and his face looked like an old black grape. He was a *gueule cassée*, one of those Great War veterans with bad facial injuries. ~~That's what Adam has told me.~~ I didn't know it at the time.

But I'm going too fast.

I was born in Port Louis at the end of the 1960s. My parents called me Melody and I'm the youngest of three. My father chose the name. He'd heard it on one of his voyages when he was at sea. "Me-low-dy," that was the way he always said it.

I had a happy childhood. I enjoyed the affection parents often save for their youngest child. I have memories of whole afternoons spent playing in the great wilderness behind our family home that served as a backyard. I used to watch columns of ants on the march. I saw weaver-birds building nests that hung from the branches of eucalyptus trees.

I wore out my sandals skipping with a rope. ~~Some people said I was a very good girl. Others said I was a bit odd.~~

But despite those early fears and wishes of mine, my life has turned out to be quite unbelievable. At the age of twenty-nine, one Saturday morning at 9:40, I died. I mean that at that moment, Melody, the person I'd been before, died, along with her husband and her son in an old white Fiat. I so loved that car. It was upholstered inside with black imitation leather. The seats sloped back too far, and the left-hand window wouldn't open anymore. The following Tuesday at 10:20 when the police officer came to my house and gave me the fateful news, my mother fainted with a great crash. But I didn't fully grasp what had happened and my first thought, my first sorrow, was for the car. I realize I loved that car the way you love a domestic animal. Later, when I finally understood the whole situation, it was a different story, of course. My grief was something terribly physical and violent. It felt just as if my head and body had been blown into little pieces but each of the scattered pieces was still alive and throbbing.

But you see, even at the worst of times you can't escape from your true nature. I've always been a dutiful wife. I wanted to give my husband, Ben, and my son, Vicky, a proper funeral. In any case I was sure I wouldn't survive them for very long. I say sure, because I didn't see how else it could turn out. Even today, I sometimes ask myself what I'm doing, still alive, here on earth. So I ordered flowers, I chose the wood and the style for the coffins. I compiled the announcements for the paper. I chose the clothes and took them to the funeral parlor myself. I wasn't able to see the two of them but, no matter, I was convinced I'd be seeing them soon enough, it was only a matter of hours. You go ahead of me, I'll soon be joining you. I've just one more thing to do down here, my dears. One last duty to perform, here on earth, one last task. To tuck you into your wooden beds. To cover you with flowers. To slip a toy, a book under your satin pillows, surround you with prayers and tell you how unfair all this is, how unbelievable it all is.

Unbelievable. And yet here I am, years later, still alive, inhaling the scent of wisteria and earth, waiting for my new family to come home.

I'm no longer called Melody. One day I saw an old film poster in a cinema. The night I checked in to a hotel room, I used the name Adèle. I took it from the poster.

I once read a story about a man who tore off one of his arms in order to escape from a mountain ravine. I've read about animals that bite off one of their paws to get out of a trap. Could it be that I have this same animal instinct for survival within me? I've killed the Melody within me and Adèle has caused me to be reborn . . .

Today I'm sitting in a house in the outskirts of a forest on the shores of the Atlantic. A little while ago I saw a grass snake and for the first time in ages I thought about my mother. And only yesterday, to soothe a sudden rise in the child's temperature, as I was giving her some medicine, I murmured a prayer. My childhood and my old ways are coming back to me. Outside, a wind has arisen, it's starting to rain. I can hear the first drops falling on the leaves. I'm thinking about Melody now. I can say this today. I can write it. I'm thinking about my old self. I'd like to say a proper goodbye to her and tell her story. Deep inside me, I haven't changed very much.

CHAPTER 2

My childhood, my adolescence. Hours, days, months, years. At 6:00 every day the kettle starts whistling. On Friday afternoons the shirts are starched. On Saturday evenings the shoes are polished as we listen to the radio. My oldest brother gets married. Six months later the younger one decides to go off to Australia. At midday on Sundays my mother cooks her famous curried fish with grilled eggplants. One Christmas Eve my father dies in his sleep in his fifty-seventh year and at 6:00 every morning the kettle goes on whistling.

At sixteen I was accepted into a secretarial school. I was an average student, except at typing. At typing I excelled. I didn't have many friends, no boyfriends. Why did I find it hard to form ties? Where did this nervousness come from?

When I left school I got a secretarial job at the bank without difficulty. My mother was so pleased! At night such silence reigned in my room that I could hear my own heart beating, and my mother breathing noisily in her sleep—her regular *puh puh puh*. What I didn't know was that every one of those moments was to be cherished. I didn't know that we ought to give thanks for light, for warmth, for the blood flowing in one's veins, for smiles, for hot meals, for a glass of cold water, for a beating heart. I didn't know.

I met Ben at the bank. My life took on new dimensions, just as my body did in my teens. It gained in harmony, joy, and laughter and I changed. I began to make plans. I stopped being afraid of the unbelievable. I forgot about my uncle's fate. I forgot that if you walk in the light too much in the end you go blind.

I'd like to rewind the course of my memory without pausing any-where. Go back to the first time I set eyes on him, when I didn't yet know who he really was, the husband he'd be, the father he'd be. When I didn't know how to read his looks, his gestures, understand his silences.

I'd like to describe him to you, how he looked, his hair, his clothes, his hands, his mouth. But I can't manage to think about him as a stranger. I think about the way he smiled when we were married. I think about the fine white kurta that he wore for his morning meditation. I think of his hands. I think of his mouth kissing me for the first time. I know I ought to be closing my eyes. I can see his are already closed, but I'm looking at this big mouth as it approaches mine and I catch sight of a brown beauty spot on his amazingly pink lower lip, and oh, I melt. I think about our wed-ding. In the very church where my father's funeral mass had been held. The benches were packed. All those aunts and cousins and uncles, all that organdy, silk, satin, lace, guipure, polyester, jersey knit, and all of it in a joyful swishing and flouncing. The singing rose and fell like a glori-ous, joyful ocean swell. I think about the two of us there, rising above all our faults, our class, our birth, promising to aim high, to do better.

CHAPTER 3

Ben worked as a cashier at a bank. It was one of the island's leading banks for what, in those days, were known as little folk. People who did not use ATMs, and could not understand bank statements printed out by machines, people who did not know how to make out a check. They needed to talk to someone who used a pocket calculator, who understood temporary difficulties, the good times and the bad. So you'd see a whole line of them passing through, fishermen, farmers, market vendors of fruits and vegetables, dressmakers, embroiderers, hardware dealers, and mechanics.

Ben and I were very happy. We'd bought our Fiat, and some furniture. We were the perfect example of the new middle class, Ben and myself, along with the thousands of other young people who squeezed into the buses and streamed into the capital. Soon, like everyone else, we'd have a house built, we'd have children, we'd buy a TV and a VCR. But Ben was not much interested in such things.

Some time before we were married he had started the Humanity movement along with four other young men—Vira, Cyril, Raoul, and Pascal. Humanity campaigned against capital punishment. The boys held their monthly meetings at our place on Saturday evenings. After our marriage we were renting a very simple house on the mountainside in the heights of Port Louis. As far as I was concerned, in the early days, they could just as well have been a group of football fans. I think I never took them seriously. But how could I have done otherwise? I knew nothing about politics and the death penalty, even though death sentences had been regularly handed down, but none had been carried out for several years.

But after three years the authorities had decided to execute a prisoner. He was Gilles Bazerte, age thirty. He'd already been in prison for ten years. One night he had used a sword to kill his wife and her parents as they slept. He was twenty then and he'd just got married. His wife was expecting their first child. She was nineteen.

By now Ben and I were no longer living in the house with gray plaster walls in the heights of Port Louis. We'd begun to leave behind the simple and sometimes happy-go-lucky life of a young couple, taking each day as it comes. We had what I liked to think was a joint project, but I was the one who wanted to do the same as everyone else, take out a mortgage, buy a plot of land, have a house built. Ben was very hesitant about moving, about leaving Port Louis. He loved it there so much. One day I managed to persuade him to visit a plot of land that was for sale in a village on the coast in the north of the country and Ben changed his mind. Was it the purity of the elements on the Saturday when we visited this plot for the first time? A blue sky, a sun as yellow as a lemon. The tall plants covered the plot with colors of gold. Was it that dirt and sand road winding through the eucalyptus trees, the Indian almond trees, the cactus and the thorny scrub that led to a little hollow surrounded by gleaming dark rocks? Was it the unbelievably soft feel of the seawater against your ankles? Was it the calm of life in that place, the birds in the trees, the wind in the leaves, the creaking chain of a passing bicycle, the motor horn from a cake salesman's van, the barking of a dog?

We were living in our new house there when the papers ran stories about the imminent execution of Gilles Bazerte. The Humanity movement sprang into action. Ben took on the role of leader, soldier, politician. Press conferences, sit-ins, demonstrations, meetings with ministers, vigils outside the prison. For three months he could talk of nothing else. But I was pregnant and more remote than ever from all this business. While Ben was fighting for a man's life I was preparing a nest.

He organized a big march from the capital to the Beau Bassin prison, where Bazerte was incarcerated. A silent, white-clad march that ended in a fight and two days' imprisonment for Ben. But Gilles Bazerte was hanged all the same, early in the morning, one Thursday at the start of winter. When the telephone rang and I heard Ben weeping I was sad that he had lost his battle but relieved that all that business was over at last. My feelings for him that gray morning were simple and sincere. My actions too: a cup of tea, a chair beside his own, a hand stroking his back. I had nothing helpful to say to him, nothing to give him courage, to lift him up again. I had no knowledge, no wisdom to help him come to terms with it all. I wonder whether he missed that.

I gave birth shortly before the end of the winter. Over there in that village in the north this was a time of cold mists in the mornings, days of hazy, faded yellow light, dark, chilly nights that suddenly swooped down. When I came home from the hospital with our little boy in my arms I noticed blue butterflies and robins in the garden. It was barely 9:00 in the morning and the summer was on its way. I remember thinking, what shall I do now?

Oh, I should have danced around with my little Vicky in my arms. I should have laughed and sung. I should have given thanks to all the gods and all the saints and filled my house with soft and joyful music.

But, of course, it doesn't occur to you to do anything like this. And so this very special day when you come back home and both of you have become parents, just when you should be starting to form the bonds for this new family, this day fades into darkness and is forgotten.

CHAPTER 4

There was a time when I had albums filled with photographs showing us at different stages of our life.

Coming out of the church on the stone steps, his arm around my shoulder, a gesture that made my veil bunch up around my head, his jacket unbuttoned. Our smiles.

In the house on the mountainside in the heights of Port Louis. I'm sitting in a plastic chair beneath the mango tree. Behind me there is a cactus with orange flowers. I never knew its name.

My mother and me in our kitchen, one Sunday. There are slices of fish on a dish, and three purple eggplants waiting to be cut up.

Me at my typewriter in the office. I have my arms crossed over my chest, I'm frowning. No one knows why. This photograph has always made us laugh.

Ben on the veranda, reading, between two anti-mosquito coils.

Vicky in tears on the hood of the white Fiat. Ben, laughing, half stretched out on the hot gleaming surface, is holding him by the waist.

Ben in front of a poster for the village elections when his movement put up three candidates.

I also had a drawer full of compilations on tape of our favorite songs. I always had a tape ready in the recorder and whenever the radio played a piece of music I liked I pressed the red "record" button.

Record: my life recorded in transparencies, photographs, tapes, trinkets. My life recorded on my skin, my heart.

This evening I shall sleep in a beautiful room on the first floor. There's a great soft bed, a warm quilt, a wooden chest of drawers, a few shelves with books on them, a pretty turquoise box on the bedside table, a lamp mounted on driftwood, old postcards of the area. My sheets smell of lavender and I have the feeling that this house is filled with wisdom, that it knows my past and my future and is helping me to recover. I like being here with them. Sometimes the four of us are all together in the living room. The two of them, the child, and me. She's curled up in her armchair, he's telling a story, the child laughs, and I'm with them, in the warmth, in shelter. Just outside the great window in the living room there are flowers growing, there's wind in the trees, the stars are shining. I feel as if the world is watching us and we make up a single, selfsame heart, living and perfect. At such moments I forget Ben, I forget Vicky, I forget that I was once called Melody.

CHAPTER 5

They dropped me off at 8:50 outside the hall where the final exam was being held for the course in "information technology and management" that I'd been pursuing for two years in order to achieve promotion within the bank. Ben had an increasingly public career. He wrote opinion columns for the papers beneath a head shot. He'd changed jobs and now had a post in the personnel department of a private bank. In the village he'd become an influential and effective local councillor. He'd been invited to the university to give a talk on capital punishment. [I sometimes had the feeling he was growing away from me and I started to be jealous of all the intelligent young women who surrounded him. What did he say to them about me? "My wife's a secretary." And, above all, how did he say it?]

It was a quick goodbye. Good luck, Melody. Good luck, *Maman*. We'll come and pick you up at 3:30. I remember Vicky's face lit up when Ben told him he could sit in front. They were looking forward to spending that day as boys together, by the sea.

At about 9:10 they stop. They go into one of the old stores beside what used to be the main highway. A dark stone building with a red corrugated tin roof. Worn paving stones on the ground, a smell of rum, iron, mildew, and rancid oil, a low, L-shaped window crammed with an odd assortment of items (colored rubber bands, pens, balls, a hammer, ropes, metal cups, remnants of cloth), a huge refrigerator with bottles of soda and beer. At the back jute sacks containing rice, dry grain, and flour. On the counter a glass jar containing candles.

In the store they order a Coke and a Fanta, which the owner's daughter serves to them with straws. According to her the boy takes a long time to finish his drink and the man has a chat with her. He asks her questions few people ever put to her and that's why she remembers them and the time at which they left. Ben asks her how long her family has had the store, what's the product that sells best, whether their trade has dropped since the opening of the self-service minimarket two hundred yards down the road, whether she'll take over the family business. He asks if they still sell cigarettes individually and when she says they do, he buys one. I know all this because the young woman called the police after the papers published the news of Ben and Vicky's disappearance. She showed them her account book, one Coca-Cola, one Fanta, one Matinée brand cigarette, one packet of chocolate Smarties.

Ben didn't smoke. I asked all his friends and his father, but they all said the same thing. Ben didn't smoke. I looked in his desk, I sniffed the clothes he wore the day before, left in the laundry basket, I looked in his shoulder bag, I searched the garden on my hands and knees. I said to myself maybe he smoked in secret at night and tossed the butts in among the plants. I didn't find anything.

The girl—her name is Julie, she was sixteen at the time—added that Ben tucked the cigarette behind his ear, shook hands with her, and drove off with Vicky at 9:40. No one would ever see them alive again.

At 9:40 I was just a back bent over a sheet of paper in complete silence and I wasn't thinking about them. At noon, when I opened my bag on a bench in the shade of a big leafy bush I don't know the name of, I discovered a little note from Ben in my lunch box. It was written in a slightly shaky hand, as if he'd been hesitant. But it was very simple: I have faith in you, good luck. No signature. No I love you, no darling. A solemn note that the police kept for long weeks before returning it to me crumpled and slightly torn on the right-hand corner.

I emerged from the hall at 3:20 and was overcome with a wonderfully giddy feeling. It was over, I was hungry, I was thirsty, I felt fine, I was knocked out. I no longer had anything left to prove. I walked lightly along to the very spot where Ben and Vicky had dropped me off. Once I got there I looked at my watch, it was 3:27. It started to rain and I opened my umbrella. The rain fell much harder, it was like uncooked rice falling in an empty cooking pot.

Now a dark road opens up before me where I wait, I spy, I survey, I start, I feel my way, I surmise, I lose my temper, I speculate, I become convinced, I lie to myself, I'm in denial, I fall over, I get up again, I presume, I act, I undo, I curse, I beg, I pray, I supplicate, I yell, I weep, and when, on the following Tuesday at 10:30, the police officer informs me that two bodies have been found in a white Fiat at the foot of the cliff near the lighthouse I start to picture things.

Their car on the old bumpy road. The solitary houses here and there, the cane fields, the tall eucalyptuses, the peacock trees, the cactuses, a doughnut stall, a stall selling yellow and red fruits. Instead of turning off to the left to go down to the sea, they take the right fork toward the lighthouse. Since we're here, why not take a look at this relic from the nineteenth century? Why not tell his son about the days long ago when they fired cannon balls, when ships sank in the open sea, when a man lived at the top of that staircase with its two hundred and twenty-three steps? It's a dreary dirt road flanked by thorn bushes. It had been raining all week and there's heavy, oozing mud that sticks to the wheels.

"Are we going to get there soon?"

"Yes, we're nearly there. It's just around the next bend. Can you hear the waves?"

I imagine it's some tiny thing that decides it. A glance at the little boy who's beginning to find the wait too long. A bend taken too sharply to the right. A steering wheel not responding quickly enough. The earth giving way and the white car sliding into the void. The waves cover up the shouts and the noise of the metal crashing onto the rocks. A wall of rain hurtles down now and rapidly erases their tracks. Sometimes I think back over all that. Not without grief. Not without tears. I'm on my bed and I can see the pine trees silhouetted against the dusk. The sky becomes tinged with pink, with orange, and sometimes there's a kind of rush of purple before the darkness envelops everything. Now I can offer Melody a calm welcome, as I now welcome the night [as this new family welcomes me]. When I remember that cigarette Ben bought and tucked behind his ear, I just hope he had time to smoke it. I like to think that on the very day of his death he wanted to try something new, as living people do.

PART THREE

The first day of winter

CHRISTMAS IS ONLY A FEW DAYS AWAY BUT WINTER HAS NOT YET arrived. The weather is gray, damp, and autumnal. Only the main streets and the boulevard beside the sea are decorated with garlands and electric snowflakes. On some afternoons there are still people surfing, and a few cafés have kept tables out on their terraces. This Wednesday morning the people getting off the buses and out of their cars are all hoping for something to happen at last; a touch of frost, a snowstorm, carol singing in the town square, a Christmas market with people selling mulled wine and toffee apples.

Adam's office is located in one of the little streets sloping down into the town center. It is early still but he has a full day ahead. He has just left a painting carefully wrapped in brown paper for room 218 at the big hotel on the seafront. He asked for a receipt. At 10:00 he is due to visit the site for what will be the biggest aquatic center in the region with the director of conurbation planning services and the project manager. The project jointly submitted by Adam's firm and another local one had been accepted scarcely a month before—a site three thousand yards square, wood heating, sauna, steam baths, Olympic pool, outdoor pool, giant chutes. The work is due to start next March and will take three years. The site is half an hour's drive from the city center, straddling a former industrial wasteland and a piece of farmland where only a few months ago there were fields of corn that reached to Adam's shoulder. If he has lunch on the way he should be back by 2:00 p.m. at the latest.

At 3:00 he is due to meet David Schtourm, the gallery owner, in the bar of the hotel. At 6:00 he has a training session with Imran. After that they will both go back to the house for a bite to eat and drink. Adèle will provide samosas. Anita has already bought the champagne.

Adam stops and takes a deep breath. That's better, he's no longer shaking at the idea of his meeting with David Schtourm, he no longer feels sick, his face is no longer plagued with nervous twitches. The gallery owner is a man who looks astonishingly like Ralph Lauren: small, gray hair, piercing blue eyes, checked shirts, his hands often in the pockets of his jeans, leather shoes with pointed toes. The list of artists he has discovered and supported is dizzying and his reputation is that of a formidable, respected, and exacting man. He has galleries in Paris, London, New York, Dubai, and Hong Kong. During the past few years he has devoted himself a great deal to contemporary art but he continues to exhibit the work of painters in traditional style whom he mysteriously unearths at all four corners of the globe and who, once they are with him, see their careers taking off like a rocket.

It is such a simple story that Adam himself sometimes finds it hard to believe. At the start of the year a business syndicate had acquired the top hotel in the city, built in 1885, and in the spring had requested bids for its renovation. The mayor of the city and David Schtourm were invited to sit on the jury. Even though his firm is too small for works on this scale, Adam had nevertheless submitted a plan and illustrated his submission with a transparency of one of the paintings from his new series. His submission was not accepted, but David Schtourm noted the illustration and wanted to know the name of the painter, and that is how Adam is now due to meet him. It was as simple as that.

When he reaches number seven Adam pauses for a moment in front of the big window through which one can see the well-ordered desk of Graziella, the firm's secretary, and that of Louis, the trainee, a first-year architectural student. Adam works in the office at the back, which has a French window leading out into a little concrete-floored courtyard, with four chairs, a table, and a big camellia in a pot on the ground. The lights in the office are on but there is no one there. Adam looks at the models exhibited in the display window and several before and after photographs of houses he has redesigned. He smiles at the Christmas tree made of flotsam that Anita had bought the previous year from a Congolese artist living in the mountains about whom she had written an article. The strips from Coca-Cola cans glitter, the stars fashioned from old lengths of cassette tape revolve gently. It is a clean, well-lit window display, but this morning it has a somewhat old-fashioned and melancholy aura. At this precise moment, when the clock on the city hall is about to strike the half for 8:30, what remains from all those years of work?

Adam has become an architect for swimming pools, conference centers, gyms, and for the local bourgeoisie. At what moment did he abandon his dreams of designing a church, a museum, a memorial? If he had not taken to painting in the secrecy of his studio, if he had given up his obsession with colors, textures, and shapes, if he had devoted all his energy and ambition to his profession, would he have become a different man, a different architect? Might he have opened an office in Paris? Might he be coming back here now merely to "move into the slow lane" and, as they say, "renew contact with the simple life" in the provinces? He suddenly thinks back, again rather wistfully, to his first years in Paris, before he met Anita. Just as his wife said she felt she was regarded as a "typical foreigner" at the cocktail parties she went to with him, so he himself felt he was viewed as a "typical provincial," with his local accent, his ungainly appearance, his local traditions, his cheese.

The light changes and Adam catches sight of his own reflection. A tall figure, stooping a little toward the window, his arms crossed over his blue parka, an old leather bag slung across his shoulder, a hazy face, much of it covered by a beard. He has a surge of affection for himself, as if for an animal that is growing old, and feeling a little lost. He uncrosses his arms and thrusts his hands into his pockets, and his fingers encounter the receipt given to him by the receptionist at the hotel that morning. Adam holds himself straight. Maybe today will be a wonderful day.

He sees Louis and Graziella returning, each carrying a cup of coffee. Adam goes into the building. "Good morning, good morning, I'm late," he says, to excuse his lack of enthusiasm for early-morning small talk. He dives into his office, closes the door.

An hour later Graziella knocks.

"Adam? Monsieur Clément's secretary has just called. He's got flu. He can't be on site this morning."

"Oh, no!"

"I'm afraid so. He's been in bed since yesterday."

"Damn! I'll call the project manager directly. Anything else, Graziella?"

"There's someone in reception for you, a Monsieur . . . hmm, wait, I've written it down. A Monsieur . . . Imam."

"An imam wants to see me?"

"No, his name is Imam. He says it's a personal matter."

"Ah! Im-ran, Graziella. For heaven's sake, it's quite simple really."

She laughs, as if she had never before heard anything so funny in her life. Adam remembers a conversation between Graziella and Louis he had overheard a few months before, and the remark: *Well, what do you expect, his wife's from Mauritius.* That evening he had told Anita about it, as it had struck him as a compliment, a little as if he had heard them saying: *What do you expect? His wife is a top model! What do you expect? His wife is a Nobel Prize winner.* But Anita, as was increasingly frequent, had hit the roof. *What's that supposed to mean? Is that some kind of flaw? A kind of fetish? Or a sickness that causes you to love only*

women with dark skin? Women from islands? Or, as you used to say,
"women of color"?

Why did she take it like that? What caused this anger? Anita
was becoming so susceptible, so touchy, so, yes, disagreeable,
sometimes. If anyone asked her where she came from, she took
it badly. If she was asked questions about her native land she
would retort that she was not employed by the tourist office. How
could she expect other people to overlook her color, her distinc-
tive nature?

When they were younger (all this seems an eternity ago to
Adam, days when they slept on a mattress on the floor, talked for
hours, made love every day, lived off pizza and processed cheese),
they had often talked about working together, creating an original artistic project. They dreamed of being the very model of
an artistic couple, mysterious, talented, and in love, they hoped
to find a new way of combining words, painting, form, color,
narrative.

Could Adèle somehow be that project? Anita is writing her
story, he is painting the same story, or at least what that story
evokes in him. A sudden anguish causes a tightening in Adam's
stomach. What were they going to do with that text, with those
paintings? How had all this taken on the form of a secret? Not a
day passes without Adam longing to puncture the abscess: all it
would take would be to sit down with Adèle and tell her everything. In simple language. *Adèle, your story has inspired us to*
write a novel, to paint pictures.

But they had never found a way of doing this and, somehow or
other, it is too late now. The novel is under way, the pictures have
been painted.

Imran is squatting in front of the Christmas tree. He gets up
when he hears Adam, but continues looking at the tree, his hands
on his hips, a posture that makes him look effeminate and child-
ish at the same time. Adam has a momentary vision of a young
lad with thick dark hair moving forward toward the starting line,

his arm held out straight before him, his body slightly stooped. Adam could tell Imran. He would understand, or at least would try to understand how Adam has gotten out of his depth with the paintings, with Anita's words, with Adèle. Imran would tell him how to extricate himself from this situation, just as he gives him advice about running, about breathing, about his footwork. Imran would not judge him.

"Hi there, Adam. Is that a Christmas tree? It looks as if it's been made out of Coca-Cola cans."

"That's exactly it, Imran. How's things?"

"It's pretty weird, isn't it? I don't say it's ugly, but why would anyone make stuff like that?"

"I guess it's a personal interpretation."

"So, how about you? Do you think it's beautiful? I guess you do. You put it up in your office."

"It's interesting."

"Hmm. Anyway, where do you buy stuff like that?"

"It was Anita who unearthed it."

"I'll bet it was. Has she written a manifesto for the preservation of Coca-Cola cans to go with it?"

"You can ask her tonight. Would you like a drink of something?"

"A coffee, if you've got time. I don't want to hold you up."

"Come along."

They are standing out in the little courtyard and Adam notices that Graziella has brought the camellia in under cover. Imran drinks his coffee slowly. It is the first time he has come to see Adam in his office and he is exhausted after walking here, exhausted by all the feelings that have been gnawing at him for more than a month and exhausted by having had to repeat his name several times to the secretary. In the old days he could have been amused by such things but he has no energy left for this. He looks at the chairs, imagines sitting on one, resting his forehead on the iron table, forgetting the weariness, the petty irritations, the pain.

Adam and Imran have known one another for a long time. As boys they used to go to the same sports club and they had more or less the same recorded times in cross-country races and the half marathon. They would run one behind the other, their sneakers filthy, their legs spattered with mud, their faces bathed in sweat. They never spoke, but now they like to think they were keeping an eye on one another.

"What's going on, Imran? Is everything okay? You're very pale."

Every Wednesday he and Adam train together, encourage one another, improve their recorded times. Then they spend a little while together for a drink or a meal. They talk about their families, their work, the passage of time, on which they are, perhaps, losing ground. It is a simple friendship, with no frills, just like the sport they both love. But recently Imran has seemed distracted, his recorded times are bad, he says he feels nauseous, preoccupied by his work. He is a mathematics teacher at a lycée on the edge of the city. Those kids, he says simply. This is enough to paint a nightmare picture, featuring six-foot adolescents who have no use for a math problem and refer to their teacher as "the Taliban" or "Massud," on account of his Afghan origin. He has not even put his name down for the half marathon at the end of February, excusing himself by saying he forgot (those kids).

"Imran? You really worry me."

Imran peers down into his coffee cup then he looks up at his friend and says softly: "Adam, I've got cancer."

A little later a man can be seen weaving his way fast through the city streets. Instinctively he seeks the sunlight, he feels cold, he is surprised by the pale, icy look of things. So winter arrived while he was at his office, maybe at the very moment when Imran was sitting down and telling him everything. Adam is thirty-nine. He needs to get back home, he needs to hug his wife and daughter tightly, he needs to forget everything he has heard this morning, he needs someone to reassure him, to give him a guarantee, someone to make him a promise, swear an oath, yes, you're going to live a long time, no, your body will not become your enemy, yes, your family will live forever, yes, your house will stand forever.

Adam drives fast and only realizes once the car has stopped outside the house that he has left his parka, his cell phone, and his shoulder bag behind. The kitchen door is open. What day is it? What did Anita say at breakfast that morning?

"Anita?"

There is indeed a woman sitting at the kitchen table, but it is not his wife, it is Adèle. She turns her head toward him and looks at him as if she were expecting him. Seeing her, he is reminded of Dutch interior paintings, a Vermeer, for example, a scene of domestic life, her flawless brown skin, her face turned toward him, her frank look, her lips hinting at a barely perceptible smile, her perfectly formed skull, her hands, repeatedly coming together and then separating in a graceful movement, the left hand tipping peas into the transparent bowl, the right dropping the empty pods onto a little green pile. Why does the presence in the kitchen of a woman other than his wife not surprise him? He ought to turn around, go back to his car, return to his office, do what he has to do, and stop acting like a child who needs to be comforted.

But Adèle is precisely what is right for him at this moment. Anita would have asked hundreds of questions, she would have been shocked that Imran has bone cancer, she would have wanted to know why *such things happen to good people*, she would have wanted to *do something*, telephone Imran, make him come over this evening, as arranged, go and see him, get him to talk, write an article on the subject, she would have clenched her fists as if it were happening to herself and she would have ended up making this "cause" her own, for with Anita, by that stage in the conversation, it would have become a "cause."

At what moment did the things about Anita that had pleased him the most begin to weary him?

"Hi, Adèle. Where are the girls?"

"Hi, Adam. Anita's gone to the paper. Laura's at her judo class. Then she's going to have lunch with her friend Sophie in the city and Anita's going to pick her up. Are you home for lunch?"

"I don't know. Maybe. Do you have something planned for this afternoon?"

"Oh yes. Anita's taking us to the lake to see the wild swans. Laura never stops talking about it. I think you saw a whole family there last year. Will you come with us?"

"No. This afternoon I have a meeting."

"Are you okay, Adam?"

The sound of the peas against the sides of the bowl, the rattle of their bedroom shutter upstairs, the kitchen door shuddering at each gust of wind, the water bubbling in the saucepan, this calm conversation about the swans, about the lake. He sits down at the table, his own wooden table, made by his father, sanded by himself, polished every week by Anita or Adèle. He feels very small, very frail, on the brink of tears.

"I've just learned that Imran is ill."

"Imran, your friend who runs like you? What's the matter with him?"

"He's got bone cancer."

Adèle stops shelling peas.

"Have you known him long?"

"Yes, since we were kids. We run together. We enter all the competitions together. When we were kids he was the only foreigner I knew. He's from Afghanistan, you know. He's very good looking, don't you think? With his very black hair that's all curly, and his eyes are as green as those peas there."

Just now Imran's eyes had seemed to him washed out, evasive. And Adam himself had been evasive, commonplace, coming out with flat, empty phrases (cheer up, old fellow!), not daring to put his arms around his friend, giving him only a pat on the back, the kind you give to losers.

Suddenly Adam begins weeping. For Imran, for himself, for this day, which should have been without any hitch, memorable, even exceptional!

Then he senses a cool hand on the back of his neck that makes him feel marvelous (had he been hot?). And he turns around to bury his tear-stained face in Adèle's lap. What happens next is automatic, biological, human, swift.

A hand moving up the back of his neck to plunge into his hair, a face pressed against a belly, then moving up and nuzzling against breasts, neck, chin, and lips. This is a woman no one has touched for a very long time and whose body, in a sudden impulse, cries out for a little male tenderness: it is a man kissing a thirsty mouth, tightly hugging a living body that is not that of his sick friend, but one that utters its secret without speaking. Adam marvels at the way his own body is awakened, becomes both more supple and harder. He now discovers another version of himself, younger, more alive, stronger, an Adam he has not been in touch with for a long time. Adèle marvels at thinking of nothing but this, at hearing herself sigh when he thrusts his head between her breasts, at being able to unzip his pants without interrupting a kiss, at rediscovering the movements you need, at not losing her way on this road. Is this being alive? Is this being cured?

The glass bowl falls to the ground, and shatters with an abrupt noise. The peas roll silently in all directions. It does not last long but it is enough to change lives.

At that moment in the city in the editorial office Anita shivers. How odd, she thinks, this sudden touch of bitter cold in the middle of the day. She has completed two pieces to appear in the local news pages and is lingering in the hope of being able to talk to the editor. It is several days now since she submitted to him pen portraits illustrating her theme of the precariousness of life in the mountains. A postal worker, a grocer, a traveling cheese salesman. People who earn just enough to keep a roof over their heads, who buy cheap meat on the last day before, or actually on, the "use by" date, who rarely go to the doctor, occasionally to the village bonesetter, but never to the dentist. Winter is now an ordeal for them since they no longer have the means to keep properly warm, their cars date from the 1980s, as do their pullovers. On New Year's Eve they watch TV and drink sparkling wine. They are under fifty but they have never found any other way to live.

Anita is sitting at the desk of a staff writer, who has gone to cover a story in Barcelona, a city in crisis for two weeks. She pictures tents pitched on the boulevards lined with palm trees, the demonstrations outside the ancient buildings, the beaches filled with people in search of different lives. Why have she and Adam never been to Barcelona, to stroll along these same shady boulevards, why have they never visited the Sagrada Família, why have they never basked on these beaches? After all, it is less than four hundred miles away. You could do it in half a day. She thinks about their friends who, over the course of a weekend, take in Prague, Florence, London, Istanbul, the way she goes and visits those godforsaken hamlets out there in the mountains and valleys. Anita pulls herself up, she ought not to say "godforsaken hamlets," she ought not to fall into the trap of scorn for what is unknown and ignored by the guidebooks, she must not think like a metropolitan liberal, is there not as much merit in writing about the postal worker eating a few lumps of sugar to overcome her hunger as in talking about the demonstrators taking over Barcelona?

"Good morning, Anita."

Christian Voubert stands there before her, his body as slim and lithe as ever.

"Oh, good morning, Christian. Did you read the portraits?"

"Yes, I've just done so. They're excellent, Anita. It's a terrific idea to present the subject from this angle. Three occupations that we generally see treated in a rather . . . how did you put it in your text . . . ?"

"As figures from folklore."

"Yes! That's it: folklore! I need a short introductory text with some numbers to set it in the context of the rest of the region, something quite simple. Can you do that?"

"Sure. What page will you put it on?"

"What do you think about the back page? With a splash headline on the front?"

Normally Anita would rush to the telephone to call her husband (*they're giving me the back page!! a full page!!*) But this is a very special day for Adam. He's due to met David Schtourm, for heaven's sake! He's been talking about it for days, wondering which painting to take, as Schtourm only wanted to see one. A few days before, in bed, he had whispered to Anita: *You do realize this could change our lives if it goes well?* How could an article in a regional newspaper compete with the prospect of a change of life? What could *equal* that?

And she's aware of it now, isn't she? Anita senses something awakening within her, something that she doesn't like, but that she takes on board without flinching. Something that resembles jealousy, dissatisfaction, provocation, and it is rather as if she were on the brink of committing an unavoidable larceny. She opens her address book, finds the number, and, as she is dialing it, recalls that office scattered with books, that copy of *Ulysses* always prominent on his desk. When he picks up on the first ring, as he always did, she smiles, amazed that he remembers her (he says, Well, I received the notices: the wedding, the birth, how old is she now, your daughter? What does he do, your husband? What are you doing yourself?) She tells him she has begun work on a novel and would welcome an opinion. He replies, very simply, Send me the opening pages, Anita.

Anita hangs up, takes deep breaths to calm her heart, stands up, looks out at the city. It was nothing, only a phone call.

It is 11:00 a.m. and the bulletins on the radio announce that it is the first day of winter at last. There is a shower of fine hail across the city. Cars skid, people slip on the ice.

Serge Clément, the director of conurbation planning services, is in bed. He is insisting that Léo must be fed. In one hand his wife holds a thermometer showing a temperature of 103 degrees Fahrenheit and with the other she calls for an ambulance. Léo, his rabbit, died when he was nine years old.

Imran is waiting in a pleasant room in D wing in the hospital. He wonders if this is the wing reserved for desperate cases, there is something falsely cheerful about the nurses, they are too well informed, they address him as "Monsieur" and his file was at the top of the pile when he arrived. The soda machine is free, they tell him. So this really must be the wing for people at death's door. He pauses for a moment in front of the window on the machine, presses 53, and a black and red can comes down. It reminds him of that Christmas tree at Adam's office and he finally decides that artifact is not so bad, after all.

At the hotel, in one of the suites with a terrace that gives a feeling of being poised above the sea, David Schtourm is lying on the bed, with Adam's painting placed beside him. At the center of the white canvas there is a great black circle, the lower part of which has run and extended beyond the frame of the picture. The four corners of the picture are spotless. This first layer of black is smooth, gleaming, and dense. It gives the impression of a skin that one could lift right off the canvas. Drops of an extraordinary vermilion red spread across this black circle from left to right. When Schtourm placed the picture on the chair beside the door and backed away as far as the window on the other side of the room, this red was transformed into a ruby necklace displayed in a black jewel case. When he studied the picture close at hand he noticed that tiny pink-and-white bubbles were trapped within the red. Here and there they had risen to the surface and had exploded into stars. These red drops (rubies, splashes of blood, pomegranate seeds, a chain of faded flowers?) had a heart, they were alive, he saw them stirring, as if the picture were not quite finished, the paint not quite dry. The gallery owner studied it for a long time, fascinated by this optical effect and by the feeling in his stomach of being inside the painting, of being underwater, of being, ever so slowly, in motion. And then he thought about something that had happened a very long time ago when he was a little boy and spending the summer in a house in the country with his grandparents. He and his grandmother had stretched out on the thick grass and watched the clouds changing, ever so slowly, from one shape into another. David Schtourm will never cease to marvel that an abstract picture can call up such a personal and precise recollection. He has several times turned the picture around in all directions, has even shaken it a little, as if he were searching for something.

As he lies there on the bed with his eyes closed, all at once it comes to him. This painting is an extract, it begins somewhere else, it does not end here. This painting is an interpretation of the present in its infinite complexity; an individual and shared present, a present that is not static, a present filled with a thousand instants, coming and exploding on its surface. David Schtourm's heart begins to beat very fast and he hears a clock striking. Eleven o'clock. Still four more hours to wait before meeting the creator of the painting that bears the title *Melody*.

The swans on the lake

ANITA IS WALKING AT RANDOM, TURNING THIS WAY AND THAT, lingering in front of splendid shop windows. She goes into several stores, spends a long time trying on a beige woolen coat she does not buy. She spins the stands containing pretty postcards at the newsagents, spends quite a while in the bookstore on the square. She contemplates the piles of books displayed on the table in the middle of the store as one might contemplate a table spread for a feast. As she is leaving, a young man stops her. He has red hair, a complexion like fresh milk. *Excuse me. Do you speak English?* Anita laughs. She has once more become that young woman of eighteen from Mauritius, strolling through a French city, marveling at the sidewalks, at a cup of steaming coffee, at red flowers on a balcony, at all the books in all the store windows, taking her time, as if the intoxication of youth, the immensity of the future, and this present were all a single entity.

In a café Anita orders a cheese sandwich and eats it at the counter while watching the whole ballet of waiters in red aprons, people dawdling in the café before returning to the office, kissing, talking, passing by. In the mirror, across from the counter, she catches her face. It looks more solid than before, as if her jaws had grown harder. She has lost the fullness of her cheeks, the rounded cheekbones. Although she likes to consider that she is free of vanity ("beauty is an inner quality" and other such nonsense) she monitors every change and could make a detailed catalog of this

131

body from head to toe, where it has slackened, been discolored, stretch marks, brown spots, a slight stoop, dryness, rolls of fat. In a few months' time she will be thirty-nine. She pays the bill, slips down from the stool with unexpected grace. It is time to go home. Who knows? Perhaps this winter will be wonderful. She pictures the possibility of receiving a whole avalanche of good news. *Those first few pages are excellent, send me the rest soon: it's high time we gave you a proper contract; the paintings will be exhibited in Paris in February; go ahead, Anita, of course you can draw inspiration from my life to write your first novel; look, Laura, the swans are there!*

After washing the kitchen floor, disinfecting and polishing the kitchen table, Adèle looks for a sheet of paper. There are plenty of notebooks and binders in this house but she would like to write her letter on a plain unattached sheet. She does not yet know what she would say in it, maybe just *forgive me*. She opens the door to the room she has never entered, where Anita sometimes shuts herself away for hours at a time. She sees the ream of paper between the computer and the printer. She moves forward swiftly with her eyes lowered, holding her breath, because she does not want to linger over the books, the bookcase, the photographs, she does not want to admire the forest through the big window, she does not want to inhale the scent of vanilla mixed with that of timber—she is no longer a part of this life, she has smashed it with her own hands, this life, but what's the use of torturing herself, she will write her letter or her single word, something, at any rate, and then leave. With two nimble steps she reaches the desk, stretches out her hand toward the stack of paper, and, in spite of herself, her gaze settles on the gray, loose-leaf binder and, oh, it's just like the one she used to use at school, she has not seen a binder like that for ages. She picks it up (simply to stroke the rough grain of the cover, to smell the scent of the pages, things you do when you come across something old) and there, underneath the binder, she discovers a pile of loose sheets neatly squared off and on the top page there is this:

The Melody of Adèle

It seems to her as if these words have no meaning, are they written in a foreign language? are they a scholarly expression?, but she does not have Anita at her side so as to be able to ask her (how many times has she done this since that first time on the beach? And always Anita replies with the same patience, *unscathed, ditto, sinecure, fallow,* the difference between a *news story* and a *filler, bimonthly, algorithm, cursive, cruciform,* the *poilus,* the *gueules cassées,* a *wartime blockhouse,* a *pine tree tapper,* a *pepper mill, rutabaga*). She opens the gray binder, recognizes Anita's handwriting.

I've started writing Adèle's book. I've been calling it that in my head for months. It's a physical being that is ever present in my thoughts, my dreams, my desires, my conversations with myself, my reading. Her presence is so extraordinary that sometimes I long for her never to go away. When she's there I feel as if she were a fountain at which I quench my thirst. This tide of words, I can't get over it. Where were they all those years when I was calling out to them? Perhaps because I had nothing to say, no story to tell? Adèle's story never leaves me now. It's as if it were my own story, my childhood, my body, my husband, my child.

Shivers run through Adèle. She glances swiftly through the rest of the binder. It is a journal kept by Anita, but there are also photographs cut out of magazines (a white Fiat, cactuses with orange flowers, a blue porcelain tea service, a typewriter), newspaper cuttings (the maloya concert, the bus accident, police raiding a factory that only employed illegal immigrants, an article on mourning), dried flowers, a sprig of lavender, a drawing of

Laura's, showing a man and two women beneath an enormous tree with heart-shaped leaves and a fairy flying above it.

Adèle hears a noise downstairs and swiftly picks up the binder and the pile of pages. She does not completely understand what she is holding in her hands but she knows it is connected to her, so it must disappear too. She has allowed herself to stray from her path, the path she had chosen so many years ago. All it has taken was a grass snake, an accident, a conversation on the beach, a ride in an old car. She picks up her black bag from her bedroom, puts the binder and the pages into it. Her actions are swift, precise. She closes the door, walks downstairs, and, as she crosses the living room, notices the paintings on the sofa.

"Are you going away?"

Adèle gives a start. Adam is there, beside the fireplace. He is crouching, bent in on himself, his arms hugging his stomach.

"Adam?"

"Are you going away, Adèle? Take this stuff with you, please. Take it all far away from here."

Adam stands up grimacing, and in a broad, weary gesture indicates the paintings on the sofa. Adèle notices his shirt is incorrectly buttoned and Adam suddenly seems to her like a giant with feet of clay, a man lost in his own body. What has happened to the flamboyant architect, the magnificent swimmer, the secret artist, the tireless marathon runner, the man who could construct both a solid house and a dream catcher as light as a soap bubble?

"Everything I've painted is for you. I've no talent of my own, you know. Look at those things on the wall, soldiers, wooden houses, beaches, water, it's all nothing. I'm just a Sunday painter, terrible daubs all my life until you came along. Take them, please. Do what you like with them. Burn them, throw them away. It's all one to me."

Adèle hugs her bag to her. Where have these paintings come from? What is that binder and that text in her bag? But as she edges toward the sofa something happens, it is like a change in

the composition of the air and the light. The paintings come to
life, the shapes move. That thick yellow circle is the winter sun
she loved so much, beside the sea on the island of Mauritius.
That black S is the march of the ants. Those are mustard seeds
about to burst open and soon their sweet and piquant scent will
fill the room. There is the blue mist that covers the mountain of
Port Louis at nightfall. This is precisely the color and shape of the
eggplant for curried fish. Here is the great wave and its foaming
spray mixed with drops of blood. Here is her childhood, her life,
her unhappiness. Here is Melody calling her back.

Adèle chokes back a cry and rushes out of the house but there
is no longer any way she can truly escape, is there? She heads
swiftly toward the forest and as she walks along, her heart and
mind are silently swimming toward that cocooned spot where
Melody has been sleeping for years.

"Will it soon be Christmas, *maman*?"

"Yes, *ma chérie*, it'll soon be Christmas. I think Papa plans to
fetch the Christmas tree on Saturday."

"Can I go with him this year?"

"Yes, I'm sure you can. You're big enough now."

"Will you come with us?"

"Well, I work on Saturdays . . . but, yes, why not? I'll fix it, don't
worry."

"So it'll be all three of us, like before?"

"Yes, like before. In the evening we'll decorate the tree with
angels and glass balls."

"Will we make cookies?"

"Yes, big cookies and heart-shaped shortbread. Look, we're
almost there."

The world is surely studded with countless such conversations,
shining like fireflies in the night. Should we not capture them in
glass jars and place them on windowsills, so as to enjoy their light
and hearken to their murmuring?

Laura is walking with her mother along a marked trail through the forest. It is cold but Anita was right not to postpone this little expedition, promised for such a long time. Adèle won't mind her not having called at the house to pick her up. When Laura had asked her if the two of them could go to the lake together, just us two, *Maman*, Anita could not refuse. That evening she will speak to Adèle, she will really try to tell her. This is her promise for the day, her New Year's resolution. And whatever Adèle's reaction and her decision, she will accept it. She will take things in hand again in the house, will stop working on Wednesdays and only exceptionally on the weekends, and will no longer rely on Adèle for everything. Anita thinks back nostalgically to Laura's first couple of years when just the two of them were together from dawn until dusk. That was good, too, wasn't it?

The sky is blue now, the path open, the cold biting. They encounter several walkers, well wrapped up like them, hi there, have a good walk. The dense light bears down heavily upon them, emphasizes the crunch of their shoes, accentuates the sweet green scent of the pine trees, ices up the fern fronds even more. Anita feels as if she were moving through one of those landscapes filmed with a special filter that reduces darkness, emphasizes contours, and polarizes colors. It is a truly beautiful winter's day.

They turn off to the right. The lake is there, bigger and more somber than they had pictured it. Mother and daughter share the same memory at that moment, a stretch of bright water in which green foliage is reflected, great flat stones at the water's edge, a wooden jetty bleached by the sun, and a laughing man diving in from it.

In the middle of the dark, waterlogged jetty stands a woman they recognize immediately. At her feet a big black bag. Each reacts differently. Anita gasps for breath. Laura utters a cry of surprise.

"Adèle!"

Adèle turns, not, as ever, with her arms open ready to enfold

Laura, but with her arms tightly folded, clutching a gray binder and some white sheets of paper. Laura lets go of her mother's hand, walks toward the jetty.

"Have you seen the swans, Adèle? Are they there?"

"Laura!"

Anita's intention had been to keep her daughter at her side, calling out to her calmly, but what emerges from her throat is an authoritarian shout. Laura stops, almost slipping over, and looks back at her mother, surprised.

"Stop there, Laura."

"But I want to see the swans, *maman.*"

"Stop there, I tell you!"

Anita walks up to the water's edge. In summer there are masses of yellow flags at this very spot. She stares at Adèle and the gray binder that she recognizes, the one she adds to almost every day, her prop, her dictionary, her memory, her box of ideas, her intimate journal. Adèle's neck, chin, and mouth are hidden by white sheets of paper, a sight that sends an icy chill through Anita's body. She does not pause to wonder how Adèle has discovered her manuscript and her binder. She does not pause to wonder why she is here on the jetty. She does not pause to wonder whether Adèle has read them. All she wants is to get them back. Now.

"What's happening, *maman*? I'm frightened."

Anita places a foot on the jetty. Adèle has not stirred, it looks as if she has not noticed Anita, her eyes are only on Laura. She wants to imprint on her memory the image of this child in a pale-pink coat, wearing mouse-gray gloves with little white stars on them, camel-colored fur boots, the soft white scarf, her eyes, her nose, her mouth, the serious, terrified expression visible in her at this moment, the curls straying from beneath her cap. In her now are all the games, all the lovely stories, all the wonder, all the promises, all the questions she asked to try to understand life.

"What are you doing there, Adèle?"

Anita's voice is sharp, full of anger, but that does not seem to affect Adèle, who goes on looking at Laura.

"Adèle. Give me that binder. Give me that manuscript."

"No, Anita. It's not yours. And where's the rest of it?"

Adèle's voice is soft as it has always been. When singing, when telling her life story, when taking orders at the Bar Tropical. A monotonous voice that Anita suddenly finds intolerable and lacking in emotion.

"The rest of what? Look, let me explain. You don't know what it is. It's a work of fiction. It's a novel."

"But the names are here. All I told you's here. So, where's the rest of the story?"

"I haven't written the rest yet! I wanted to talk to you about it, Adèle, I promise you I was going to do it. Tonight, actually! Give it back to me, please, Adèle. GIVE ME BACK MY THINGS!"

Adèle backs away, shaking her head, and Anita begins shouting.

"You know nothing about it, Adèle! You've never read a book in your life. You don't know what it is. Who do you think you are? You don't exist. You've got no papers. No family. You're nothing!"

Anita stops, stunned by the viciousness of her own words. Her body is leaning forward, her fists are clenched, as if she were preparing to strike Adèle. She tries to calm down, she takes deep breaths, summoning up positive thoughts, happy memories, she closes her eyes. Hush, hush, remember, Anita, only yesterday you still loved her, this woman, you wanted her to stay in your house forever, to look after your child, so that you can go out into the world and write articles about forgotten people, the poor, the unhappy, the exploited, and dine out off your tales of their world. Remember, you liked to hear her singing to your daughter the very nursery rhymes that your mother used to sing to you, but that you say you've forgotten, remember how you love her coconut cakes, her banana doughnuts, her curried fish, her green papaya salad; remember how she calmly told you her personal story because you questioned her, because you asked her for details; you told her, you must talk, Adèle, you must emerge from your mourning; you told her you're in a deep depression and only words can help you emerge from that. Remember how every morning you promised you would tell her everything and accept her reaction. Remember your daily cowardice.

The two women are not so very far apart. They both grew up under the same tropical sun, they like the same food, the same music, they speak the same language, they have lived beside the sea but have never learned to swim, they could have been sisters. Anita opens her eyes and it is suddenly Melody that she sees, barefoot, her body convulsed with trembling, her mouth emitting a strange gurgling sound. Anita's legs give way, she crouches on the jetty, desperate, exhausted. That voice in her head, the one that is forever in search of the telling detail, the color, the brand, the word, the thing out of place, the tic, the odd one out, the dust motes in the light, the random flow of tears according to the grain of the skin, the voice that had on one occasion dredged up from the depths of her memory a green plastic apple used for storing balls of cotton, that same voice now said: *Adèle stood barefoot on the slippery jetty, she did not know why she was there but she knew she had arrived at the end of her road.*

Anita begins weeping because she is suddenly so tired and so appallingly shocked to have heard herself saying and thinking such things—you never know what you are capable of, how many times has this been said to her and only now, close to the age of forty, has she plumbed the depths of her selfish and imperfect heart. Anita weeps with relief too, all right, let it end now, let her take the binder, take the manuscript, and go.

At this moment, now that everything has gone quiet, another way still remains for each of them, there is still another door they can open. They can separate here, as calmly as they had met. One of them can take her daughter's hand and go home to her wooden house. The other can disappear once more, survive or not.

Suddenly.

"Adèle, give *maman* back her things. That's her work. You're being wicked!"

Almost before Anita has time to turn round, Laura rushes forward. At the very same moment, or just a fraction earlier, a shout is heard from among the trees.

Adam follows Adèle at a good distance behind her. She plunges into the forest, not once looking back, with a sure tread. When she reaches the lake she takes off her shoes to walk onto the jetty. Adèle takes something from her bag and moves into the middle of the jetty. She sits down cross-legged with her back to him and bows her head over what she has taken out of her bag. Is it a book? Is it a photograph? After several minutes Adam retreats a little into the woodland, locates a fallen tree, and sits down on it. From time to time he stands up to check that she is still seated there, her head bowed forward. Perhaps she has finally relaxed a little.

There in the icebound forest, he slowly recovers his spirits, at last he can breathe. This is what he will do: watch out to ensure nothing happens to Adèle, she seemed very strange just now, her eyes dilated, the pupil had covered up the iris. Thinking about this, he unties his shoelaces, one never knows . . . What possessed him to show her those paintings like that? When she has finished here (reading, looking, contemplating) he will take her back to the house, will speak calmly to her and make her understand that what happened this morning (her body, so broad, so soft, so all embracing, her scent of fresh soap) will not be repeated. He will tell her she is safe here, that the choice is hers, she can leave, she can stay. Yes, that's a good beginning. In an hour's time everything can be as it was. He can pick up the threads of his life, get a grip on himself, for heaven's sake! Telephone David Schtourm to apologize, telephone Imran to say something other than platitudes, and arrange to spend the New Year's weekend away somewhere (Barcelona, for instance) instead of staying at home. Wood, the fire, the family, hot chocolate, and the Christmas tree scenting the evening are no longer enough, he must pull himself together. Anita is right, he is on the brink of turning into an old stick-in-the-mud. He thinks about that Christmas tree with its strips from Coca-Cola cans and smiles. Tomorrow he will shave off his ridiculous beard.

Suddenly he hears voices and his heart misses a beat.

"But what if the swans aren't there, *maman*?"

"We'll come back another day. But I'm sure they will be. They come every year, you know."

Anita and Laura are quite close to him, walking past him, hand in hand, and for several seconds he has a vision of them as nymphs slipping between the trees, destined to live for a long time and to love him forever.

Later on when Adam is in his cell, with long blank hours stretching out ahead of him, he will ask himself why he remained hidden like a thief, instead of showing himself to them.

Adam feels as if his head is about to explode. Of course, the swans! Adèle knew as well, is that why she has come here? Is she thinking of telling Anita everything? Adam would like to rewind time, run in the other direction, return to the house, yes, sit down at the kitchen table, act as if nothing had happened, as if he knew nothing. Yes, no, yes, no, he becomes as agitated as a caged lion there among the trees, which barely a few moments ago had seemed to offer him some kind of salvation. He feels stupid, he has failed on all counts, he is nothing but a selfish, flawed bastard. He bends down to tie up his shoelaces and that is when he hears the shouting.

Anita and Adèle are on the jetty and he recognizes the gray binder in Adèle's hands, the famous gray binder that always stays at the house, and that no one is allowed to touch. Laura is about to scramble onto the jetty as well, a little pink figure. Deep inside him a wild and primitive awareness senses what is about to happen. This terrible instinct beats a path up to his mouth and

brings out a feral but perfectly useless howl that does not stop
Laura and does not warn Anita but causes Adèle to retreat to the
end of the jetty.

It takes several seconds.

Laura has a child's impulsiveness, she does not have the patience to wait, she does not understand everything, she has seen
her mother's tears, she has heard the argument. She has recognized the binder (so many times her mother has said to her, Don't
touch that! That's my work). At this moment what Laura wants is
to get it back, to drive away Adèle, who is making her *maman* cry,
and win praise for this good deed. She believes she can achieve
this the way she believes she can climb onto the wisteria arbor
without falling, or that she could fly if she had wings attached
to her back. Deep down inside her she simply wants Adèle to go
away for a while, a little while, so that things might be just as
they were before, when her parents belonged only to her and she
belonged only to her parents. She rushes forward. She is eight.

Adèle draws back, closes her eyes, and opens her arms, con-
fronted by the little girl in pink hurtling toward her. The binder
falls, the sheets of paper cascade like angels' wings. All it takes
to determine her fate is the thrusting gesture of an angry child's
little hand. She throws up her arms as if heading for death via a
back somersault. It is much easier than she had imagined. Her
body hits the water and she slips slowly into this dense cold world,
just as she has so many times pictured the white Fiat slipping
down the cliff. She no longer thinks of anything and, as Anita
had so truthfully said, she is nothing, she does not exist.

When Adèle falls into the water, Laura utters a cry and takes
a step sideways to regain her balance (she can distinctly hear her
judo teacher's voice: legs apart, knees bent!) but her foot slips on
a sheet of paper, her ankle twists, she skids, her head hits a post
but she feels no pain. The little figure tumbles over into the lake.

As for Anita, just before plunging into the water herself, and even though she has seen everything, and even though she, too, rushes in with a shout, and even though she cannot hear Adam yelling, for in truth no sounds exist anymore, she makes this unforgivable gesture, this downward lunge with an outstretched arm, as if to retrieve something and as she jumps into the water her fist is already grasping her gray binder. Long afterward, when the newspapers praise her courage and her maternal impulse to save her daughter from drowning, even though she herself cannot swim, she will think about that gray binder in her hand and, if there were nothing else to send her straight to hell, her place there would be well earned.

Adam is howling and running at the same time. Is this the perpetual stride that marathon runners speak of, this dissociation between body and mind? His body is an implacable machine but his head is on the point of exploding with distress: whom to save first, whom to search for first, his wife or his daughter? He is not thinking of Adèle, at this moment she no longer exists. The air grows denser, the light explodes in red showers, he is howling like an animal. Yet once he sets foot on the jetty and dives from it as he has done so many times, his mind and body are fused into a fierce and speedy ball of energy. If there is to be only one it will be Laura.

A kind of truth

ADAM IS SITTING ON A METAL CHAIR CLUTCHING A MUG OF BURNING-hot coffee in his hands. He is calm, he is ready. He has learned the story by heart. Now it is his story. The police officer, who has a lean face, without warmth but with no malice, looks at him. There is an extremely orderly desk between them. A laptop computer, a spiral-bound notebook, a jar of pencils, a roll of Scotch tape, a stapler, a ruler, and a little ebony elephant that Adam finds exquisite.

"Tell me again what happened back there."

"I've already told you several times. I've told your colleague, I've told the emergency services."

"I know. But I need to hear the story again."

Did he emphasize the *s* in the word *story*? Adam must not let himself be distracted. Adam must not waver.

"We went to the lake to see the swans."

"There are swans on the lake?"

"Yes. Last year we saw a whole family. There were nearly ten of them. My daughter wanted to see them again."

"Was it normal for Adèle, that is to say the woman who called herself Adèle, to go with you like that on family outings?"

"Yes."

"Why?"

"She was one of the family."

"And you'd been sleeping with her."

"Yes."

"For how long?"

"Six months. Maybe longer."

At the hospital when Laura was in intensive care Adam and Anita had again become what they had been one day long ago on a green sofa: two minds animated by a single desire, the same wish to be brave, to give the best of themselves. They had decided to tell a story in which their eight-year-old daughter would play no part, in which they would not have to explain the complex nature of their relationship with Adèle. No novel, no paintings. Just a humdrum tale of infidelity that ended badly and, according to Alexandre, their lawyer friend, who went to see them before they were questioned by the police, things like that happen much more often than you'd think.

"Your wife knew?"

"No."

"And your daughter?"

"Certainly not."

"Are you positive? You never know for sure what goes on in children's minds. Maybe she'd already seen you with Adèle."

"No! Laura didn't know."

"Okay. Go on."

"We'd just got to the lake and Adèle threatened to tell my wife everything."

"Just like that? All of a sudden? Were you planning to dump her or kick her out?"

"No."

"Maybe you were going to denounce her?"

"Denounce her? I don't understand."

"She was an illegal immigrant, wasn't she? You knew that and yet you employed her for years."

"Yes, I knew that, but I didn't intend to denounce her. I don't know why she wanted to reveal everything. I've no idea."

"And then?"

"I managed to get her away from my wife and daughter. I didn't want them to hear what we were saying."

"You mean, two weeks before Christmas that would have been a bit of a disaster."

"Things got very heated. She started shouting and I wanted to shut her up."

"You wanted to kill her?"

"No! No! Never! I just wanted her to keep quiet but she began struggling and fell into the water."

"You pushed her."

"No! I don't know. I don't know anymore. I was horrified. I didn't want her to spoil everything, but she started struggling and then she fell. The jetty was very slippery."

"Your wife and daughter: where were they at that moment?"

"They heard the argument and came over. My daughter ran up to me. She slipped. She . . . she . . . Laura. Laura."

Adam thinks back to that moment with dazzling clarity, just before his body hit the water. Laura first. Laura above all. He had reached Anita first (to whom could he one day confess his rage and despair at reaching her, his wife, first, and not Laura?) and a few seconds later he had brought Laura up to the surface. At the hospital they estimated that Laura had been underwater for less than three minutes. Three minutes? How can life contain so many emotions, decisions, and changes of mind in less than three minutes? Adam begins shaking.

"Calm yourself, Adam."

"I need to see my daughter. It's hours now since anyone gave me news."

"She's still in a coma."

Adam curls up on his chair, clutching his stomach, biting his lips so as to avoid weeping. He sways back and forth. This is a nightmare. What else could it be? This should have been a glorious day.

"Just one more thing and then you can sign your statement."

"What?"

"Were the swans there?"

Yes, they had been there. While Anita was running back to the house to telephone the emergency services, Adam was hugging his daughter to him, his ear pressed to her mouth, listening hard to the feeble breathing he could hear, never letting go either of this body nor of this feeble breathing. Out of the corner of his eye he thought he had seen something moving on the lake. For one magical moment he thought Adèle was emerging from the water. But then he heard the great clatter of wings and said softly to Laura: *Look, ma chérie, the swans are there.*

Anita is lying on a mattress in her daughter's room. Alexandre has just informed her that Adam will be kept in a cell and brought before the magistrate the next day. Anita had thought of offering an apology for the occasion when she virtually called him a racist but what would be the point now? Those things, those words, those evenings no longer matter. She feels ill. She had not stopped vomiting. In her house, after telephoning the emergency services (surrounded by the order and perfection of this house, the paintings, the books, the box of toys); in the ambulance; in the hospital corridors. Anita gets up, holds her daughter's hand, a cold, limp little thing, and takes a deep breath. Amid the eerie hissing of all the apparatus she decides to get a grip on herself. This is what she will do: take a shower, eat something, remain alive, look after her daughter, remain resolute. She has no concept of the fact that this is exactly what she will be doing every day for the next four years, five months, and thirteen days.

Far away from all this David Schtourm has just dined in a discreet, old-fashioned restaurant in the upper part of the city. He likes cities beside the sea, he likes certain things to remain traditional (restaurants, hotel lobbies, service, the furniture in bistros), he likes the mist that softens the biting cold, he likes the hazy yellow halos around the streetlights on the promenade. He thinks about the painting back in his room, the hour he spent waiting for that artist-architect who never came. He could leave the painting at the hotel reception the next morning before catching his flight, he has the address of the architectural firm, but, as he is walking back to the hotel, he decides to keep the painting because, above all, he would like to know both the beginning and the end of this story.

Further away still, François Sol is thinking about Anita. He smiles as he recalls with affection that young woman who was playing at being somebody else. And yet she had something about her, that girl. I wonder what she has done with it, he muses, as he turns to his copy of *Ulysses*.

Today

ADAM LEAVES THE PRISON AT 12:15. AS HIS LEFT FOOT SETTLES UPON the little square of yellow grass in front of the gray prison gates, he recalls how much he used to love the month of June. He is astonished at such notions from the old days, these notions of a free man; prison has taught him to expect nothing, to hope for nothing other than what he had been given the day before. Back in his cell it made little difference whether it be February or June, the hours were there, solid, massive, and silent.

He moves away from the square of dry grass. The parking lot where Anita is waiting for him is a little farther on, tucked away around to the right, but suddenly he stops. He would so like to be at his best today. He will not permit his fears, his anguish, and his sadness to rise to the fore. He tries to summon up positive thoughts, as the prison psychologist has advised him to do; today he is going to be reunited with Anita, take Laura in his arms, go back home, saw wood, swim

Swim.

All at once the lake begins to intrude on his thoughts. The vision recurs of Anita, Laura, and Adèle on the jetty and he still remembers the colors of their coats. From where he stood, cowering among the trees, they made him think of brushstrokes— red, black, pink. Oh, for heaven's sake, was he so self-obsessed, did everything always come down to painting, to his accursed painting? The images from that terrifying day crowd in on him like famished and thirsty beings of flesh and blood. He steps back and finds himself once more on the square of yellowed grass. Then he thinks of his gray-and-white cell, the clusters of light on the wall in the morning, the impeccable order of things inside the prison, the sofa bed, the table, the chair, the books all lined up, the right angles, the colored pencils in a jam jar, the drawing books stowed away in a portfolio. He has been learning to breathe slowly, through the nose and the abdomen. Sometimes this deep breathing has been putting him into such a profound state of meditation that he had the sensation of being back home in the forest. He should do this now, it will calm him.

Suddenly there is a noise like a great blow struck against the gate behind him. And Adam is running. It is the last lap of the marathon. Twenty-six miles or four and a half years, what's the difference?

The asphalt turns into a carpet of mud, the cars disappear, it is a pine forest, the gray building is no longer there, it is a holiday, with smells of caramelized sugar, rain, sausages, and another two hundred yards to the finish. Anita is waiting there behind the yellow ribbon that will enwrap the winner. She is carrying Laura, barely two years old, on her shoulders. Anita is beautiful, it is there for all to see, that bewitching beauty, that voluptuous figure (in reality those eight pounds she has been unable to shed since Laura was born). As everyone waits for the marathon runners to arrive, amid this cheerful, impatient crowd, all eyes are on her, her smile, her blue summer dress, her fine fingers clasping the ankles of the child she carries, straight back, head held aloft. It is Laura, perched up there, who sees her father emerging in front as they come around the bend and who yells *PAPA*!

Adam is coming, yes it is definitely him, those smooth strides can only be his, that towering body, made for basketball but fine for running (and for so many other things). He hears that *PAPA* and some people claimed that at that moment his stride took on a new life, as if he had found a little bit more energy to increase his speed. Adam flings his arms wide open to meet the yellow ribbon, Anita runs up to him, leans toward her husband, and in a movement of perfect grace, Laura tumbles into her father's arms. The onlookers feel as if they have witnessed something flawless, timeless, and invincible.

Today in the prison parking lot there is only Anita waiting for him. Laura has remained at home, being looked after by a health care assistant. Adam buries his face in his wife's hair, now dappled with gray. This gray touches him and suddenly there is the scent of vanilla, there, behind her ear and he is amazed at the butterflies coming to life in his stomach. He closes his eyes, remembers a goddess in a blue dress, and their daughter gently tumbling, light as a bird, into his arms and this thing that blazed up in his body, cauterizing his pain, sharpening his joy in victory, this thing that made him feel what it was to be a man loved, a man envied, a god.

Tomorrow

ON WEEKDAYS DURING THE SPRING, THEY CAN SOMETIMES BE SEEN on the beach where the wartime blockhouses are. They come halfway through the morning, settle down on beach towels, open a great blue sunshade. They never swim. Occasionally they take a walk near the concrete blocks. At such times the man carries the girl on his back. Sometimes they dip their child's feet into the clear rivulets that wind around the concrete blocks and take her hand so that she can stroke the velvety moss on the walls of the pillboxes.

People around here know them and even if it was a long time ago there is always someone who can tell their story. But mostly when people see them like that with their daughter, they prefer to look away and think about other things.

The girl is very tall, she has long, smooth hair, she is too thin. Because she uses a wheelchair, and because she sometimes starts yelling, nobody apart from her parents notices the exceptional beauty of her face nor the way her eyes reach down into your soul.

They still live in that big house on the edge of the forest and, since returning from prison, the man spends his days repairing, consolidating, and making things. Some people remember that he had been an architect and a painter and the same people have the notion that while he was in prison his wife sold some of his paintings to pay for their daughter's medical treatment. He has converted his former painter's studio into a cabinetmaker's workshop where he makes, repairs, and transforms furniture. He is a much-sought-after craftsman who receives visitors by appointment only. It is said that the floor in his workshop is covered in a thick layer of dried paint reminiscent of a multicolored carpet.

The woman still occasionally writes articles for the local newspaper under a pseudonym. She no longer goes to the fourth floor of that humdrum building the color of rough plaster, nowadays she telephones Christian Voubert on his direct line and he suggests topics to her. Sometimes she says yes, sometimes she cannot see the point of it. In her study these days there is not much literature. She devotes a good deal of time to reading books about drowning and coma, scientific studies on the psychological effects, accounts by survivors. She keeps herself informed about new developments in the cases of children suffering from neurological aftereffects. She is constantly on the lookout for new institutes, new medications, research in progress, clinical trials, hypnosis, herbal treatments, essential oils, miracles.

It is only in the evening, when Laura is asleep, that Adam and Anita can sit side by side together once more. They will talk softly about the day's events. The gutter repaired, the furniture polished, the complete meal Laura has managed to eat, her progress with physical therapy. They never go beyond such tangible things. They hold fast onto these real things so as not to stray out of their depth. Of course the memory of Adèle often hovers between them, but the truth is that by that time in the evening they have not much energy left for her.

At this stage Anita and Adam simply want the day to end and for all thoughts, wishes, and regrets to close up for the night like water lilies. They go to their bedroom, lie down in silence. Before switching off the light they kiss and say to one another, till tomorrow, then.

AUTHOR'S ACKNOWLEDGMENTS

A big thank-you to the American artist Ed Cohen who allowed me to draw inspiration from his magnificent paintings as well as his working technique for the character of Adam. His paintings can be seen at www.edcohenstudio.com.

Thanks to my parents, to Anuradha Roy, Christel Paris, Davin Appanah, Elsa Lafon, Jean-Philippe Rossignol, Monique Gouley, Myriam Greisalmmer, Xavier Houssein.

TRANSLATOR'S ACKNOWLEDGMENTS

I am indebted to a number of people, and especially the author, for their advice and assistance in the preparation of this translation. My thanks are due, in particular, to my editor at Graywolf Press, Katie Dublinski, and to Thompson Bradley, Daphne Clark, Robin Dewhurst, June Elks, Martyn Haxworth, Simon Strachan, Susan Strachan, and Cherry and Paul Thompson.

Nathacha Appanah was born in Mahébourg, Mauritius. She is the author of *The Last Brother*, which has been translated into sixteen languages. She works as a journalist and translator and lives in France.

Geoffrey Strachan, who also translated *The Last Brother* into English, is a prizewinning translator of works from both French and German, including novels by Andreï Makine, Yasmina Reza, and Jérôme Ferrari.

The text of *Waiting for Tomorrow* is set in Kepler Std. Book design by Ann Sudmeier. Composition by Bookmobile Design & Digital Publisher Services, Minneapolis, Minnesota. Manufactured by Versa Press on acid-free, 30 percent postconsumer wastepaper.